The Christmas Swap

A holiday they won't forget!

Nurse Luci Dawson and Dr Cal Hollingsworth have both had their lives turned upside down. So when they get the chance to swap houses in the run-up to Christmas it could be just what they need to start afresh for the festive season!

Find out what happens in:

Waking Up to Dr Gorgeous
by Emily Forbes

and

Swept Away by the Seductive Stranger
by Amy Andrews

Available now!

Dear Reader,

When I was asked to write a duo with Emily Forbes centring around a house swap I leapt at the chance. I simply adored the movie *The Holiday*, and thought the concept would be great to play around with. There are no snowy cottages or Jude Laws in this one, but there *is* Outback Australia, a delicious wounded doc and a no-nonsense small-town nurse who's super-wary of love—particularly when it comes in the form of a very temporary locum.

I was also thrilled finally to be able to put a train in a book! In 2012 my husband and I travelled on the Indian Pacific from Sydney all the way across the country to Perth, and I have been wanting to put that trip in a book ever since. Growing up as the daughter of a railway man, I've always felt trains are in my blood, and some of my happiest childhood memories involve train trips with the family. There's just something so romantic about saloon cars, moonlit landscapes flitting by, and two strangers making love all night to the clickety-clack of the rails against the track.

I hope you enjoy the journey through this book as much as I did bringing it to you.

Happy reading—and all aboard!

Amy

SWEPT AWAY BY THE SEDUCTIVE STRANGER

BY
AMY ANDREWS

Published in Great Britain 2016
By Mills & Boon, an imprint of HarperCollins*Publishers*
1 London Bridge Street, London, SE1 9GF

© 2016 Amy Andrews

ISBN: 978-0-263-06552-7

Printed and bound in Great Britain
by CPI Antony Rowe, Chippenham, Wiltshire

Amy Andrews is a multi-award-winning, *USA TODAY* bestselling Australian author who has written over fifty contemporary romances in both the traditional and digital markets. She loves good books, fab food, great wine and frequent travel—preferably all four together. To keep up with her latest releases, news, competitions and giveaways sign up for her newsletter—amyandrews.com.au/newsletter.html.

Books by Amy Andrews

Mills & Boon Medical Romance

Visit the Author Profile page at millsandboon.co.uk for more titles.

To my dear friend and colleague Emily Forbes.
It was a blast—let's do it again some time!

CHAPTER ONE

CALLUM HOLLINGSWORTH WOULD have had to be completely blind not to notice the sexy blonde in his peripheral vision. Thanks to a combination of excellent medical care, the passage of time and her being on his right, he wasn't.

Although it was her laugh he'd noticed first.

She was talking on her phone and even though her tone was hushed her occasional laughter practically boomed around the busy café. It was so damn...unrestrained, so carefree, he couldn't help but stare.

Callum hadn't had much to laugh about in recent times and a hot streak of envy tore through his chest as he ogled her from behind his sunglasses. Long honey-coloured hair with curly ends that brushed her shoulder blades. A glimpse of sun-kissed skin at her throat and on toned, tanned arms. Legs clad in denim that were shapely rather than skinny and knee-high fringed boots that looked more country girl than dominatrix.

She didn't wear any make-up or jewellery. In fact, there was a lack of anything flashy or ostentatious about her yet she shone like a jewel in the old-fashioned café in Sydney's Central Station as the sun streamed in through the high windows overhead.

Maybe it was the way she laughed—with her whole body—that held his attention. Maybe it was the jeans and the boots. Maybe it was her lack of pretension. Whatever, he was just pleased to be provided with some relief from the burden of his thoughts as he sat waiting for his train to depart.

For God's sake, he was about to embark on one of the

great train journeys of the world. He was leaving Sydney and going somewhere else for two months where nobody knew him or about the tumble his career had taken. He could reset the clock. Reinvent himself.

Come back refreshed and show them all he didn't give a damn.

The sooner he got to grips with his old life being over, the sooner he could get his act together. This was his chance to finally get his head out of his backside and work on being impressively happy once again. Because he sure as hell was sick of himself and the dark cloud that had been following him around for the last two years.

Nothing like moving fourteen hundred kilometres away to send a strong message to himself about the new direction of his life.

'All passengers for the Indian Pacific, your train is now ready for departure from platform ten.'

Callum gathered his backpack at the announcement over the loudspeaker. The woman on the phone crossed her legs and kept talking and a pang of disappointment flared momentarily. She obviously hadn't been waiting for the same train. Visions straight from a James Bond movie of a glamorous night between the sheets with a mystery woman on a train as a brilliant way to kick-start his new life fizzled into the ether.

He gave himself a mental shake, his lips twisting at the insanity as he headed towards the exit to the platforms.

A thrill of excitement shot through Felicity Mitchell's system as she stepped into the luxurious carriage and was ushered to her compartment by a man in a smart uniform who had introduced himself as Donald, her personal attendant. She passed several other compartments with their doors open and smiled at the couples who beamed back at her.

Booking a double suite in platinum class on the Indian Pacific was a hideous extravagance. She could have done the

Sydney to Adelaide leg in the sitting compartment or even the gold class and saved a lot of money, but it had been a lifelong dream of hers to watch the world chug by as she lay on her double bed, looking out the window. She'd spent the last of her inheritance on the fare but she knew her grandpa, wherever he was now, would be proud.

They passed a compartment with a shut door before Donald stopped at the next one along. 'Here you are,' he said, indicating she should precede him.

Felicity entered the wood-panelled compartment dominated by a picture window. A small plate of cheese and biscuits sat on a low central wooden table. A long lounge that would become her double bed sat snugly against the wall between the window and a narrow cupboard where her bags had already been stowed.

'This is your en suite,' he said, opening a door opposite the lounge to show her the toilet and shower. It was a reasonable size considering the space constraints.

Donald gave her a quick run-down on her compartment and other bits of information about the service before asking if she'd like a glass of wine or champagne as the journey got under way.

Would she? *Hell, yeah.*

'Thank you, Donald, I would love a glass of champagne.'

He smiled at her. 'One glass of bubbles coming up.'

Felicity waited for him to leave before she danced a crazy little jig then collapsed onto the lounge in a happy heap. Workers scurried around on the platform outside, ready for the train's departure in a few minutes. She couldn't believe she was finally sitting in this iconic train about to begin the trip of a lifetime.

Donald returned quickly and handed her a glass full of fizz. 'You're just with us until Adelaide, that's right, isn't it?'

'Yes, that's right. I'd love to go on all the way to Perth. Maybe one day.'

The Indian Pacific was so called because it travelled the

width of Australia between the Indian and Pacific oceans. The full trip from Sydney to Perth took three days. Her leg of the journey was only twenty-four hours.

'I think you'll enjoy yourself anyway,' Donald said.

'Oh, yes,' Felicity agreed. 'I have absolutely no doubt. I've been looking forward to this for most of my life.'

'So, no pressure, then?'

Donald laughed and Felicity joined him as the train nudged forward. 'And we're away,' he said.

Felicity looked out the window. The platform appeared to be moving as the train slowly and silently pulled away. 'Let me know if you need anything. Dinner's served at seven.'

Felicity nodded then turned back to the window, sighing happily.

Felicity emerged from her compartment half an hour later. She'd stared out the window, watching the inner city give way to cluttered suburbs then to the more sparse outlying areas as it headed for the Blue Mountains. And now it was time to meet her fellow travellers.

Her neighbour's door was still firmly closed as she headed out. Maybe she didn't have one yet. Maybe they'd be joining the train at a later stop? Quelling her disappointment, she headed for the place she knew people would be—the lounge.

And she hit the jackpot. Half a dozen couples smiled at her as she stepped into the carriage, her legs already adjusted to the rock and sway of the train. She stopped at the bar and ordered a glass of bubbles from a guy called Travis. It was poured for her immediately and she made her way over to the semicircular couches where everyone was getting acquainted.

'Hi,' she said.

The group greeted her as one. 'Sit down here with us, love,' said an older man with a Scottish accent. The woman with him moved over and made some room. 'If you don't

mind me saying so, you don't exactly look in the same demographic as the rest of us.'

Felicity laughed. 'I have an old soul.'

Every other person in the lounge would have to have been
in their sixties. At twenty-eight that made her the young-
est by a good thirty years. Luxury train travel was clearly
more a retiree option than a hip, young, cool thing to do.

But that was okay. She'd never been particularly hip or
cool. She was a small-town nurse who genuinely liked and
was interested in older people. She had a bunch of oldies at
the practice who she clucked around like a mother hen and
she knew this lot would probably be no different despite
what would be a short acquaintance.

'What do you do, dear?' a woman with steel-grey hair
over the other side of the lounge asked.

Felicity almost told them the truth but a sudden sense
of self-preservation took over. If she told them she was a
nurse, one of two things would happen. She'd have to give
medical advice about every ache, pain or strange rash for
the next twenty-four hours because, adore them as she did,
too many people of the older generation loved to talk ob-
sessively about their ailments. Or they'd pat her hand a lot
and tell her continually that she was an angel.

If she was really unlucky, both would happen.

She might be a nurse but she was no saint and certainly
no angel. In fact, that kind of language had always made
her uncomfortable.

And she didn't want to be the nurse from a small community where everyone knew her name on this train journey of a lifetime. She didn't want to be the girl next door.
She wanted to be as sophisticated and glamorous as her
surroundings. She wanted to dress up for dinner and drink
a martini while she had worldly conversations with complete strangers.

Nursing wasn't glamorous.

'Oh, I'm just a public servant,' she said, waving her hand

dismissively as she grabbed hold of the first job that came to mind. She doubted it was very glamorous either but it was one of those jobs that was both broad and vague enough to discourage discourse. Nobody really understood what public servants did, right? They certainly didn't ask them about their jobs.

Or tell them about their personal medical issues.

'What do you do?' Felicity asked, and relaxed as the woman, called Judy, launched into a spiel about her job of forty years, which kicked off a conversation amongst them all about their former jobs, and that segued into a discussion about the economy and then morphed again into chatter about travel.

Felicity was in heaven. She was on a train surrounded by witty and enthusiastic companions on the inside and the rugged beauty of the Blue Mountains on the outside. For twenty-four hours she was determined to be a different person.

Tomorrow afternoon she'd be back home where everyone knew her name and stopped her in the street for advice about their baby's fever, their weird allergies or their shingles. Where everyone called her 'Flick' and the guys called her 'mate' and the older women of the town tried to matchmake her with any remotely available male.

Tomorrow would be here soon enough. Today nobody knew her and she was going to revel in it for as long as she could.

The first thing Callum noticed when he entered the restaurant at seven sharp was the sexy blonde from the café. He blinked once or twice just to make sure it was her—his vision wasn't the best after all. Then she laughed at something her companions were saying and it went straight to his chest and spiked through his pulse.

It was definitely her.

If he'd known she was in the platinum carriage too he

wouldn't have wasted the last few hours catching up on some essential reading his new boss had emailed and insisted he read before he started work.

'Can I find you a dining companion, sir?' Donald asked.

'No,' Callum said. The beautifully dressed tables seated four and there were several spare chairs around the elegantly appointed dining car but his gaze was glued to the empty one beside her. 'I've found one.'

The corner of Donald's mouth lifted a fraction. 'Good choice, sir.'

It took him only a few more seconds to reach the empty chair next to blondie. 'Excuse me,' he said. The conversation stopped as all three diners turned to look at him. 'Is this seat taken?'

Her eyes widened slightly. They were smoky grey and fringed by sable lashes. She stared at him for long moments and he stared right back. He liked that she seemed as confused by her reaction to him as he was to her.

She'd changed into a dress, a slinky black thing that showed off her neck and collarbones and crisscrossed at her cleavage. She was wearing lip gloss. Pink. Light pink—the colour of ballet shoes. The ends of her honey hair seemed curlier or maybe that was just a trick of the overhead light.

The old guy sitting opposite welcomed him heartily. 'Sit down, young fella. Save this pretty young thing from having her ear bent off by us old fogies.'

Callum didn't wait to be asked twice. He wasn't someone who believed in instalove but he sure as hell believed in instalust. He may be rusty but he knew sexual interest when he saw it.

She sure as hell wasn't looking at him with pity, like too many women had these past couple of years.

No more pity sex for him.

'I'm Jock, this is my wife Thelma and the odd one out is Felicity.'

Callum shook Jock and Thelma's hand and reached for

blondie's. *Felicity.* 'Nice to meet you,' he murmured, their eyes meeting again, an awareness that was almost tangible blooming between them.

'You were in the café,' she said after a beat or two, sliding her hand out of his.

He let it go reluctantly. 'Yes.' A purr of male satisfaction buzzed through his veins. She remembered him. Had she been checking him out at the same time he'd been ogling her?

'I didn't realise you were in the same carriage.'

'I had some work to do.' Callum grimaced. 'I shut myself away for a while. I'm in number eight.'

'Hey, you're in nine, right?' Jock asked Felicity jovially. 'You're neighbours.'

Callum smiled at her as he sent a quick thankyou up into the universe. Things were definitely looking up for him. She smiled back and for the first time in a long time his belly tightened in anticipation. His libido had taken a real battering since the accident, so it was a revelation to feel it rousing.

'So, what do you do?' Jock asked.

Callum dragged his gaze off Felicity and forced his attention on the couple opposite. She wasn't the only person on the train and this was the way these social situations worked. You ate a good meal, drank good wine and made polite and hopefully interesting conversation with strangers.

God knew, he needed something like this to get himself out of his head. But he promised himself that later he would do his damnedest to shamelessly monopolise the woman beside him. They might not end up in bed together but he intended to flirt like crazy and see where it went.

'I'm a technical writer,' he said.

The well-practised lie rolled smoothly off his tongue. He still wasn't used to the real answer. Becoming a GP after being an up-and-coming vascular surgeon was taking some getting used to. And he only had to look around at the age demographic of the other passengers in the carriage to know that admitting to being any kind of doctor would probably result in an avalanche of medical questions he just didn't want to answer.

He didn't want to be any kind of doctor tonight. He wanted to forget about the bitter disappointments of his career and just be a regular Joe. He wanted to be a man chatting to a woman hoping it might end up somewhere interesting.

'Oh?' Thelma asked, as she buttered the bread roll Donald had just placed on her plate. 'What does that entail?'

'Just boring things like industry articles and manuals,' he dismissed. 'Nothing exciting. What about you, Thelma? Are you still working?'

It was a good deflection and Thelma ran with it. The conversation shifted throughout the sumptuous three-course meal and it felt good to stretch his conversational muscles, which were rusty at best. Felicity, on the other hand, was a great conversationalist and Callum found himself relaxing and even laughing from time to time.

His awareness of her as a woman didn't let up but the urgency to get her alone mellowed.

Like him, she seemed reluctant to talk about herself, expertly turning the conversation back to Thelma and Jock or himself and more neutral topics, such as travel and movies and sport. Consequently, the meal flew by as Felicity charmed them all. It was hard to believe he'd sat for two hours and not thought once about the accident and its repercussions on his life.

That wasn't something *anybody* had achieved in the past two and a half years.

He went to bed thinking about it, he woke up thinking about it, and it dominated his thoughts far more than it should during the day.

He suddenly felt about a decade younger.

'A few of us are retiring to the lounge for some after-dinner drinks,' Jock said as he placed his napkin on the table. 'I hope you'll both join us.'

'Of course,' Felicity said, smiling at their companions before turning that lusciously curved mouth towards him. 'You up for that? Or do you…have more work to do?'

Callum wanted nothing more than to invite her back to his compartment for some *private* after-dinner drinks. Their gazes locked and her cheeks pinked up and he wondered if she could read his mind. She was a strange mix of eagerness and hesitancy and Callum didn't want to push or embarrass her.

But he could see in those expressive grey eyes that she didn't want him to lock himself away again either.

'I'd love to,' he said, resigning himself to sharing her for a bit longer, to go slowly, to drag out a little more whatever it was that was building between them.

Anticipation buzzed thick and heavy through his groin.

Felicity found it hard to concentrate for the next couple of hours, aware of Mr Tall-Dark-and-Handsome sitting beside her in a way she hadn't been aware of a guy in a long time. Every time he spoke or laughed it rumbled through his big thigh pressed firmly against hers and squirmed its way into her belly.

There was a sense that they were marking time and she was equal parts titillated and terrified. This being a whole other person thing wasn't as easy to pull off as she'd thought but she'd never felt so alive either. So utterly *buzzed*.

Not even with Ned. Sure, he'd been the love of her life and being dumped by him had been crushing, but their love had grown out of friendship and a slow, gentle dawning.

This…*thing* was entirely different.

Was she seriously going to do this? Pick up a stranger on a train? Or let *him* pick her up? She might have limited experience of the whole pick-up scene but she was pretty sure that's exactly where they were heading. When she'd booked her train ticket, meeting a good-looking stranger hadn't been part of her plan.

But here they were with a night full of possibilities stretching ahead of them.

One by one their companions left, withdrawing to their beds, making jokes about old bones and early nights. Felicity contemplated doing the sensible thing and following them. Retiring to her bed and the moonlit landscape flying by outside her window, tuning into the clickety-clack of the wheels as they rocked her to sleep.

But she didn't.

'Well,' Jock said, standing, helping Thelma up as well. 'This is way past our bedtime and my indigestion is playing up so we'll be off too.'

Felicity smiled at them and bade them goodnight, excruciatingly conscious of Callum's eyes on her as she watched their companions disappear from the lounge.

And then there were two.

'Whew,' he murmured, his gaze brushing over her neck and mouth, a smile tilting his lips into an irresistible shape. 'I thought they'd never go to bed.'

Felicity blushed but she didn't deny the sentiment. She'd thought exactly the same thing.

He tipped his chin at her martini glass. 'Another drink?'

She hesitated. This was it. This was the moment. Was she going to be the sophisticated woman on the train or the girl next door?

'It's only eleven,' he coaxed. 'I promise to have you back to your compartment before you turn into a pumpkin.'

Oh, God, oh, God, oh, God. The man had a PhD in flirting. 'Yeah. Okay. Sure.'

He grinned. 'Good answer.'

Felicity's mouth quirked in an answering grin. 'Good question.'

She flat-out ogled him as he walked to the bar. She'd seen him in the café and had been struck by his presence but he'd seemed so brooding and intense, so closed off she hadn't bothered to go there. He hadn't put a foot wrong tonight, however.

Sure, there was still a brooding quality to the set of his shoulders and the line of his mouth, but he'd been witty and charming and great with all the oldies and, good Lord Almighty, the way he'd looked at her had been one hundred percent high-octane flirty.

Nothing brooding about it.

Even the way the man leaned against the bar was sexy. His expensive-looking charcoal trousers pulled nicely against his butt and hugged the hard length of his thighs.

And they *were* hard. And hot. She could still feel the imprint of them along her leg.

He'd worn a jacket to dinner but had since shed it to reveal a plain long-sleeved shirt of dark purple. The top two buttons had been left undone and about an hour ago he'd rolled up the sleeves to reveal tanned forearms covered in dark hair.

Those forearms had caused a cataclysmic meltdown in her underwear.

He turned slightly and smiled at her and Felicity sucked in a breath. The man was devastating when he smiled and it went all the way to his green eyes. It did things to his face, which was already far too handsome for any one man. Square jaw covered in dark, delicious stubble, strong chin, cheekbones that women would kill for and sandy-brown hair longer on the top and shorter at the sides.

Hair made to run fingers through.

His laughter drifted towards her as Travis handed over the drinks and said something she couldn't quite hear. She liked how it sounded. How it rumbled out of him. She got the sense he didn't do a hell of a lot of it, though, which was a shame. That laugh was turning her insides to jelly.

The military should employ him as a secret weapon.

He headed in her direction, his gait compensating for the

rock of the train. She probably should be glued to the window, watching the moonlit bush whizzing by, and not be so obvious, but she figured they were beyond the point of being coy and, frankly, he was too damn hard not to look at with his long stride and knowing smile.

He placed her glass down and sat opposite her this time, a low table between them. She couldn't decide if she was relieved or disappointed. Neither, she concluded as he filled her entire field of vision and everything else became pretty much irrelevant.

'To strangers on a train,' he said, lifting his whisky glass, that smile still hovering.

She tapped hers against it. 'I'll drink to that.'

CHAPTER TWO

FELICITY WAS CONSCIOUS of his gaze as it followed the press of her lips then lowered to the bob of her throat as she swallowed. She was grateful for the cold, crisp martini cooling her suddenly parched mouth.

'So…what's a *young 'un*—' he injected Jock's Scottish brogue into the words and Felicity smiled '—like yourself doing on a train with the cast from *Cocoon*? Lots more people your age down in the cheap seats. Unless… Wait, are you some kind of heiress or something?'

'No.' Felicity laughed at the apt description of their travelling companions and at the thought of her being some little rich girl, although she had inherited enough money from her grandfather to buy a small cottage. 'I'm not. And you don't look like you're of retirement age either. You're, what? Thirty-five?'

She'd been wondering how old he was all night and this seemed like as good an opener as any.

'Close,' he murmured. 'Thirty-four. And you?'

'Twenty-eight.'

'Ah…' He gave a long and exaggerated sigh. 'To be so young and carefree again.'

Felicity laughed at his teasing but was struck by the slight tinge of wistfulness. 'Oh, no,' she teased back. 'You poor old man.'

He grinned at her and every fibre of her being thrilled at being the centre of his attention. 'Seriously, though,' he said, sobering a little, 'why the train?'

'My grandfather was a railway man through and through. Fifty years' service as a driver and he never got tired of trains. Of talking about them, photographing them and just plain loving everything about them. We'd go on the train into the city every day when I used to stay with them in the school holidays and he'd take me to the train museum every time without fail.'

He frowned. 'Didn't that get boring after a while?'

Felicity shook her head. 'Nah. He always made it so exciting. He made it all about the romance of train travel and I lapped it up.'

'Romance, huh?' He raised an eyebrow as his gaze dropped to her mouth. 'Smart man.'

Felicity's belly flopped over. 'That he was.'

If tonight was anything to go by, her grandfather was a damn genius.

She stared into the depths of her frosty glass as her fingers ran up and down the stem. 'He spent his entire life saying that one day he was going to take my grandmother on the Indian Pacific for a holiday of a lifetime. Then, after my grandmother died when I was twenty, he used to tell me one day he and I would go on it together. He died last year, having never done it, but he left me some money so…here I am.'

The backs of Felicity's eyes prickled with unexpected tears and she blinked them away.

'Hey.' His hand slid over hers. 'Are you okay?'

'God, yes,' she said, shaking her head, feeling like an idiot. *Way to put a downer on the pick-up!* 'Sorry. I didn't mean to get so maudlin. I'm stupidly sentimental. Ignore me.'

'Nothing wrong with that.' He smiled, removing his hand. 'Better than being cold and hard.'

Felicity returned his smile. She appreciated his attempt to lighten the mood. Sometimes, though, she had to wonder. If she was a little more hard-hearted she probably wouldn't fret so much about her patients or become so personally involved. It would make it much easier to leave it all behind at the end of the day.

'What about you?' she said, determined to change the subject. To get things back on track. 'Why the train?'

'I guess I'm a bit like your grandfather. Always loved trains. Doing all the great train journeys of the world is a bucket-list thing for me and when I had to travel to Adelaide I thought, Why not?'

It was stupid to feel any kind of affinity with a man—this man—because he was a train guy. Especially when up until about eight hours ago she hadn't even known him. But somehow she did. Her grandfather had always said train people were good people and, even though he'd been biased, right at this moment Felicity couldn't have agreed more.

Callum was ticking *all* her boxes.

'So...' He took a sip of his whisky. 'Felicity...'

Goose-bumps broke out on her arms and spread across her chest, beading her nipples as he rolled the word around his mouth. She'd never heard her name savoured with such carnal intensity. It sure as hell made her wonder what it would sound like as he groaned it into her ear when he came.

Lordy. Another box ticked.

'Is that a family name?'

She cleared her throat and her brain of the sudden wanton images of him and her twisted up in a set of sheets. 'Nope. My mother just liked it, I think. And I don't really get called that anyway.'

'Oh?' He frowned. 'You get Fliss?'

Felicity grimaced. 'Flick, actually.'

'Flick.'

He rolled that around too but it didn't sound quite the same as when he'd used her full name. She didn't hate the nickname, she'd never known anything else, but she didn't want to be a Flick tonight.

Tonight she wanted to be *Felicity*.

She shrugged. 'My cousin couldn't pronounce my full name when she was little and it stuck.'

He lazed back in his chair, his long legs casually splayed

out in front of him, the quads moving interestingly beneath the fabric of his trousers. 'You don't look much like a Flick to me,' he mused.

Felicity's pulse fluttered as she suppressed the urge to lean across and kiss him for his observation. The sad fact was, though, in her everyday life she did look like a Flick. Her hair in its regulation ponytail, wearing her nondescript uniform or slopping around in her jeans and T-shirt.

'Thank you,' she murmured, raising her glass to him and taking a sip.

'My brother calls me Cal.'

Felicity studied him for a moment. 'Nope. You *definitely* don't look like a Cal.'

'No?'

Felicity smiled at the faux wounded expression on his face. 'No.'

'What *do* Cals look like?'

'Cals are the life of the party,' she said, happy to play along. 'They're wise-cracking, smart-talking, laugh-a-minute guys. You're way too serious for a Cal.'

He laughed but it wasn't the kind of rumbly noise she'd come to expect. It sounded hollow and didn't quite reach his eyes. *Crap.* She'd insulted him somehow. Way to turn a guy off, Flick.

She had to fix it. *Fix it, damn it!*

'Anyway,' she said, hoping like hell she sounded casual instead of panicked. Nothing like ruining their evening before it had progressed to the good bit. 'I like Callum. It's very…noble.'

A beat or two passed before he laughed again, throwing his head back. It was full and hearty with enough rumble to fill a race track. It rained down in thick, warm droplets and Felicity wanted to take her clothes off and get soaking wet.

The laughter cut out and he fixed her with his steady gaze. 'Just so you know, I'm not feeling remotely noble right now.'

Felicity's belly clenched hard and she swallowed. *Eep!* This was really going to happen. He downed his whisky and put the glass on the table. 'Would you like to come back to my compartment?'

She cursed her sudden attack of nerves. But this wasn't her. She didn't do this kind of thing. Could she pull it off?

'Hey,' he said, leaning forward at the hips and placing his hand over hers. 'We don't have to. I just thought…'

Yeah. He'd thought she was interested because she'd practically done everything but strip her clothes off and sit in his lap. *God, she must look like some freaked-out virgin.* Or some horrible tease.

Felicity could feel it all slipping away. She didn't want to pass this up, damn it, but she hadn't expected to feel so… conflicted about it when it came to the crunch.

So she did what she always did in lineball calls. She picked up her phone.

He quirked an eyebrow at her. 'What are you doing?'

'I'm asking Mike what he thinks I should do.'

A bigger frown this time. 'Mike?'

'Yeah. You know, the guy in my phone who talks to me and tells me stuff like why the sky is blue and where the nearest hairdresser is.'

He chuckled. 'Yours is a dude?'

She shrugged. 'You can choose and Mike sounds like Richard Armitage so it was a no-brainer.'

'And do you always let your phone decide such things?'

'Sometimes. It's the modern-day coin toss, right?'

He chuckled again. 'Well, this ought to be interesting.'

Felicity grinned as she pushed a button and brought her phone up closer to her mouth. 'Mike, should I go back to Callum's?'

The phone gave an electronic beep then a stylised male voice spoke in a sexy English accent. 'Is he good enough?'

They both laughed then he grabbed her wrist and brought the phone closer to his mouth. Her pulse point fluttered madly beneath his fingers as their gazes locked. A smile played on his mouth again as he spoke into the microphone, his eyes firmly fixed on her. 'He's very good, Mike.'

Felicity's toes curled in her pumps at the sexually suggestive reply. *That wasn't what Mike had meant.*

'Does he know how to treat a woman?'

He didn't laugh this time, just eyed her intently as he replied. 'Oh, yeah. He knows *exactly* how to treat a woman.'

'Then you don't need me to decide, Felicity.'

He released her hand, slowly, still holding her gaze with a red-hot intensity. 'Looks like the ball is in your court.'

Felicity's heart tripped as he fixed her with a gaze that left her in no doubt they were both going to be naked within about ten seconds of the door shutting. Her breath hitched but she was aware of Travis, still at the bar, in her peripheral vision.

What would he think if they left together? Would he gossip about it with the rest of the crew? Would everyone know in the morning that she and Callum had spent the night together?

If she was back home in Vickers Hill, *everyone* would know.

But she wasn't. Was she? She wasn't *Flick* here. She was *Felicity* and *nobody* knew her.

Felicity picked up her glass and swallowed the last quarter in three long gulps. She stood, her body heating as his lazy gaze took its sweet time checking her out. 'Your compartment or mine?'

He smiled, downed the last of his whisky and held out his hand. She took it, smiling also, tugging on his hand, impatient now she'd taken the first step to get on with it.

Jock entered the lounge at that moment and Felicity halted, letting go of Callum's hand immediately, like a guilty teenager. The older man was in a pair of tracksuit pants and a white singlet.

'Jock,' she said, smiling as she walked towards him,

aware of Callum close on her heels. 'Thought you'd be in the land of nod by now.'

Jock gave them a tight smile. 'So did I but…' He rubbed his chest. 'My indigestion is really giving me hell tonight. I thought I'd come and ask Travis for a glass of milk. That usually does the trick.'

Felicity felt the first prickle of alarm as she neared Jock. The subdued night-time lighting in the lounge hadn't made the sweat on his brow and the pallor of his face obvious.

'Jock?' She frowned. 'Are you okay?'

Callum stepped out from behind her, also frowning. 'You don't look very well.'

'You need to sit down, I think,' Felicity said, ushering him over to the closest chair.

'Do you have any cardiac history?' Callum asked as Jock swayed a little, reaching for the arm of the couch.

'No. Never had any ticker prob—'

Jock didn't get to finish his sentence. He grabbed his chest and let out a guttural cry instead, folding to his knees.

Adrenaline surged into Felicity's veins. *'Jock!'* she said, throwing herself down next to him.

But it was too late. He collapsed the rest of the way, splayed awkwardly on the floor. Felicity gave him a shake but there was nothing.

'He's having an MI,' Callum said as he helped Felicity ease Jock on his back.

Felicity blinked at the terminology. An MI, or myocardial infarction, was not a term a layperson used. Nonmedical people said heart attack. 'He doesn't have a pulse,' she said, feeling for his carotid.

'Oh, my God, what's wrong with him?' an ashen-faced Travis asked, hovering over them.

'I'll start compressions,' Felicity said, ignoring the bartender as more adrenaline surged into her system and she kicked into nursing mode.

'He's in cardiac arrest,' Callum said as he automatically

moved around until Jock's head was at his knees. Felicity admired the steadiness of his voice and the expert way he tilted Jock's jaw and gave his airway support.

Technical writer be damned.

'Do you guys keep a defib?' Callum demanded. 'Some kind of first aid kit? We need more help. And we need to figure out how to get him to an ambulance.'

Felicity couldn't agree more. She had no idea if that was possible but she knew they couldn't keep him alive indefinitely. Jock needed more than they could give him here on a luxury train in the middle of nowhere.

Things were looking grim for the travelling companion she'd grown fond of in just a few hours.

'Yes. We have a defib,' Travis said, his voice tremulous as Felicity counted out the compressions to herself. 'But I've never actually used it on a real person before.'

'It's fine. I'm a doctor,' Callum said, his voice brisk.

Felicity glanced at Callum, not surprised at the knowledge given his use of medical terminology and his total control of the scene.

'And I'm a nurse.'

He glanced at her but didn't say anything, just nodded and said, 'Go,' to Travis as he leaned down and puffed some breaths into Jock's mouth.

It was satisfying to see Jock's chest rise and fall. CPR guidelines had changed recently, focusing more on chest compressions for those untrained in the procedure. But for medical professionals who knew what they were doing airway and breathing still formed part of the procedure.

And old habits died hard.

Callum's training took over and all his senses honed as he rode the adrenaline high, doing what he did best—saving lives. Travis was back in under a minute, bringing a portable defibrillator, a medical kit and the cavalry, who arrived in varying states of panic. He tuned them all out as he grabbed the defibrillator, turned it on, located some pads, yanked up Jock's singlet and slapped them on his chest.

Even Felicity in her dress and heels, pumping away on Jock's chest beside him, faded to black as he concentrated on Jock. Once this was over—which could be soon if they couldn't revive Jock—he'd think about her being a nurse. About how they'd both lied. For now he just had to get some cardiac output.

Felicity stopped compressions while the machine was reading the rhythm. Callum opened the medical kit, relieved to find an adult resus mask. At least he could give Jock mouth to mask now.

The machine advised a shock.

'All clear,' Callum said, raising his voice to be heard above everyone talking over everyone else.

Felicity wriggled back. So did he as the room fell silent. The machine automatically delivered a shock, Jock's chest arcing off the floor.

'Recommence CPR,' the machine advised, and they both moved back in, Felicity pounding on the chest again as he fitted the mask and held it and Jock's jaw one-handed.

'Where's the nearest medical help?' Callum demanded of a guy with a radio who appeared to be the head honcho.

'We're about twenty clicks out of Condobolin. Ambulance will meet us at the station. A rescue chopper is being scrambled from Dubbo.'

'How long will it take to get to Condobolin?'

'The driver's speeding her up. Fifteen minutes tops.'

Callum wasn't sure Jock had fifteen minutes, especially if he wasn't in a shockable rhythm. He wished he had oxygen and intubation gear. He wished he had an IV and access to fluids and drugs. He wished he had that ambulance right here right now. And a cardiac catheter lab at his disposal.

But he didn't. He had a defibrillator and Felicity.

He glanced at her. He didn't have to ask to know she was thinking the same thing. Fifteen minutes was like a lifetime in this situation, where every second meant oxygen starvation of vital tissues.

'Piece of cake,' she muttered, a small smile on her lips, before returning her attention to the task at hand.

He smiled to himself as he leaned down to blow into the mask. There was controlled panic all around him, with orders being given and radio static and the loud clatter of wheels on the track as the train sped to Condobolin. Somewhere he could vaguely hear poor Thelma sobbing. But amidst it all Felicity was calm and determined and so was he. Fifteen minutes? He'd done CPR for much longer.

'Check rhythm.'

Felicity stopped so the machine could do its thing. When it recommended another shock they followed the all-clear procedure again and once more the entire lounge fell silent, apart from Thelma's sobs.

Jock's chest arced again but this time it was successful.

'Normal rhythm,' the machine, no bigger than a couple of house bricks, pronounced.

Felicity gasped, a broad smile like the rising sun breaking over her face. 'I've got a pulse,' he confirmed, grinning back. 'Jock?' Callum pulled the mask away. 'Can you hear me, Jock?'

Jock gave a slight moan and made a feeble attempt to move a hand. 'Jock? Jock!' Thelma threw herself down beside them.

'Is he okay?' she asked, looking first at Callum then at Felicity through puffy red eyes.

'We got him back,' Callum said. Both of them knew he wasn't out of danger but it was something.

Felicity reached across and squeezed Thelma's arm. 'He's still very unstable,' she said gently. 'But it's a good sign.'

Callum was relieved when the train pulled into the station, even if the strobing of red and blue lights around the iron and tin structure of the roof created a bizarre discotheque. Very quickly a drowsy Jock was transported out of the train to the ambulance, accompanied by a paramedic, Callum, Felicity, Thelma and the rail guy with the radio.

Finally Callum had access to oxygen and a heart monitor. It was worrying to see multiple ectopic beats and runs of ventricular tachycardia, though, and Callum crossed his fingers that Jock's heart would hold out until he got the primary cardiac care he so urgently needed.

Callum and the paramedic whacked in two large-bore IVs and then Felicity was helping Thelma into the ambulance and he was getting in the back with Jock. There was no question in his mind that he'd stay with the old man and hand over to the medivac crew when they landed at the airstrip in approximately fifteen minutes' time.

He glanced out the back window as the rig pulled away, the siren a mournful wail in the deserted streets of the tiny outback town. Felicity was framed in the strobing lights, staring after the ambulance. She looked exactly the way he suspected they all probably looked. A little shell-shocked as the adrenaline that had ridden them hard started to ebb.

But also strong and calm. As she had been throughout.

This was not how he'd pictured tonight would end, and as the mantle of regret settled into his bones he knew their moment had passed.

He watched her with a heavy heart until she faded from sight.

CHAPTER THREE

FELICITY LAY AWAKE on her bed an hour later, staring out the window. The train was still stationary at Condobolin station, which was in darkness after the ghoulish flashing of emergency lights. Her compartment was also in darkness, except for the slice of light coming in from the hallway through her open door.

Callum hadn't returned and she couldn't sleep.

After the ambulance had disappeared she'd gone back to her compartment and showered, standing beneath the spray shaking like a leaf as the adrenaline that had sustained her during the emergency had released her from its grip.

She'd waited around in the lounge for a while after they'd gone, thinking Callum would be back soon. Some of her fellow passengers joined her, curious to know what was happening, but they didn't linger and eventually Donald had urged her to go back to her compartment and try and get some sleep.

But she couldn't. It was hard to shut her brain down after what had transpired.

She was about to give up, switch her light on and grab a book out of her bag when Callum strode by her door.

'Oh…hi,' he said, obviously surprised to see her awake and her door open as he pulled up short. She'd deliberately left it ajar because she didn't want to miss his return.

Felicity sat up and swung her legs over the side of the bed. 'You're back.' She stood and took a couple of paces towards him, conscious, as he took up all the space in her doorway, of how different she looked now in loose yoga pants and T with bare feet, compared to the high-heeled, little-black-dress woman he'd been flirting with earlier.

He looked exactly the same. Only sexier. His calm and control when everyone else around them had been losing their heads had kicked his good looks up to a whole other level.

Why was competence so damn attractive?

'How's Jock? Did the medivac transfer go smoothly?'

'Not really. He went into VF while we were waiting for the plane and we had to shock him twice to get him back.'

Felicity pressed her hand to her mouth, a hot spike of concern needling her. 'I was worried something was going down. You were gone so long.'

'I stuck around and helped them stabilise him for transport.'

'Of course.' They'd have wanted to have everything as controlled as possible before they loaded him on the chopper to avoid any chance of midair deterioration. 'What are his chances, do you think?' she asked, folding her arms.

'I don't know. He's not very stable at the moment. It's a forty-minute chopper flight to Dubbo hospital and by that time he'll be about ninety minutes post–cardiac tissue injury. He's inside the window, so fingers crossed, with some tertiary management he should be okay. I'll check on him when we get into Adelaide tomorrow.'

Felicity nodded. 'I guess we're going to be kind of late into Adelaide.'

'I guess we are. Although Donald reckons they'll be able to make up a lot of the time.'

'I'm in no hurry,' she said, and gave him a smile because she could stay on this train and look at him for a decade and it probably still wouldn't be long enough.

He smiled back, his gaze locking with hers. 'Neither am I.'

There was silence for a beat or two while they just stood and smiled at each other in some weird moment of shared intimacy as only two people who'd been through such a high-stakes ordeal could.

The train moved forward unexpectedly and jostled him inside the compartment, bringing him a step closer. He ducked his head down to glance out the window. 'Looks like we're off.'

'Yes,' Felicity said, as she half turned to find the darkened station platform appearing to slowly move.

When she turned back he was staring at her with heat in his eyes. They'd been flirty earlier but now they were just plain frank. His gaze dropped to her mouth as he took a step towards her. Her breath hitched. The atmosphere thickened and pulsed with promise.

She'd resigned herself to this not happening but suddenly it was on again.

'So...' She swallowed to moisten her suddenly parched throat as he loomed big and broad and close enough to reach out and touch. '*Not* a technical writer, huh?'

He cocked an eyebrow. '*Not* a public servant?'

She shrugged. 'I didn't want to be regaled with a dozen different medical stories or be canonised as some kind of saint.'

'You're forgetting about the lectures on the state of the health-care system.'

She laughed. 'Those too.'

Felicity supposed she should ask him more about his medical background but right now she didn't care. Not with her pulse fluttering madly at her temple and warmth suffusing her belly. 'You were great out there.'

'So were you.'

'Not quite what I expected would happen tonight.'

He smiled. 'Me neither.' And then, 'Are you...okay? It was kind of intense. The adrenaline was flowing.'

'Sure, steady as a rock.' Felicity held up a hand horizontally. It betrayed her completely by trembling.

'So I see.'

Felicity glanced from it to him, conscious of the sway of the train. Conscious that she was far away from Vickers Hill.

It emboldened her.

'That's not from the accident.'

Her hand was trembling for reasons that were far more *primal*.

He regarded her for long moments before turning slightly and reaching for the door behind him to shut it. He turned the lock with a resounding click, the noise slithering with wicked intent to all her secret places.

They were truly alone now.

Darkness pressed in on her, the only light entering from the strip at the bottom of the door and the moonlight pushing in through the window. It was enough to allow her eyes to adjust quickly.

Enough to see Callum.

He turned to face her, stepped closer, so close his breath warmed her forehead. He reached for her hand, which had fallen by her side. 'Maybe you just need to...' he slid her hand onto his chest, flattening it over his heart, his big hand holding hers in place '...grab hold of something solid?'

Felicity dropped her gaze to their joined hands. Each thud of his heart reverberated through her palm, scattering awareness to every cell of her body. She'd never had a one-night stand or done anything so spontaneous. But on a night when she'd been reminded how precarious life could be she needed it.

She needed this. She needed him.

The clickety-clack of the wheels on the track faded. 'Maybe I do,' she murmured, the scent from his citrusy cologne filling her senses until she was dizzy with wanting him.

Like a slice of lime after a shot of tequila.

His kiss, when it came, was gentle. So gentle it almost

made her cry. It was long and slow and sweet. It was everything she hadn't known she needed in this moment.

Earlier, if she'd been asked how this would go down, she would have said fast and furious. But this was infinitely better. Burning slow and bright, building in increments that piled on top of the next, making her yearn and ache and want even as it soothed and sated.

His hands slid around her waist. Her arms snaked around his neck. He drew her closer. She lifted up onto tiptoe.

Their hearts thundered together.

When he finally pulled away, they were both breathing hard. His eyes roved over her face, glittering with the kind of fever that also burned in her. What was he looking for?

Permission. *Sub*mission?

He had it.

'I knew you'd taste this good,' he muttered, the low, husky rumble stroking right between her legs.

His next kiss wasn't long and sweet and slow. It was hot and fast and dirty. Just as she'd imagined it would be. His lips were firm and insistent, his tongue seeking entry, which she gave him on a greedy moan. His hands slid under her T-shirt, tightening her belly and heating her blood to well past boiling.

She was so damn hot and horny she could barely see. She certainly couldn't think. All she could do was feel. And surrender.

Her bra snapped open and she gasped and pressed into his palm when his hand cupped a breast.

'God,' he murmured against her mouth. 'You feel good.'

Felicity moaned as his thumb taunted her erect nipple. 'Don't stop.'

He did, but only temporarily as he whisked both her T-shirt and bra off. 'Oh, yes,' he muttered, as he drank in the sight of her bare breasts, one hand sliding around her back, pulling her closer as he lowered his head to the opposite nipple and drew it deep into the warm cavern of his mouth.

Felicity sucked in a breath, her back arching, her hand sinking into the silky softness of his hair. His mouth tugged relentlessly at the nipple and it was equal parts delicious and dangerous. A tingling between her legs built with every hot swipe of his tongue as if he was licking her there instead.

Just then the train clacked loudly and jostled them apart as it got up to speed. Felicity held on to him, her hands curling around his biceps as their bodies lurched to the movement. His hard thighs bracketed hers, steadying them.

Hell. She'd forgotten she was even on a train. The noise of the wheels on the track and the sway was something she'd quickly become accustomed to.

And nothing outside the havoc of his mouth had registered.

'How about we get horizontal?' he suggested, his lips buzzing her neck, his big hands anchored to the small of her back. 'Before we injure ourselves?'

Felicity laughed at the imagery of them being found by Donald in the morning sprawled on the floor, her still half-naked.

God, this was totally insane.

She couldn't believe she was doing it. Getting down and dirty in her train compartment with a comparative stranger.

It was exciting and titillating and scandalous and there was nothing she wanted more.

She slid her hands onto his and eased them off her, keeping hold of him as she walked backwards the two paces required to reach her bed. The backs of her thighs hit her mattress and she sat down, looking up at him, their hands still joined.

She eased her legs apart slightly and was thrilled when he stepped between them. He released himself from her grip and cupped her face with both of his hands.

'You're beautiful,' he murmured.

'You're not so bad yourself.' There was a classic beauty

to the angle of his jaw, the blade of his cheek, the cut of his mouth.

Lordy, that mouth.

He smiled, his fingers burrowing into her hair. 'Lie back.'

Felicity shook her head as her gaze zeroed in on his fly, which was, most conveniently, at eye level. 'Soon,' she muttered, reaching out to walk her fingers along the thick bulge testing the strength of his zipper.

He sucked in a breath and a dizzying hit of sexual power surged through her system.

'I don't think that would be a good idea,' he said, but the subtle increase in pressure through his finger pads on her scalp betrayed his true desire.

'You don't like?' she asked, blinking up at him with as much innocence as she could muster.

'Oh, no,' he said with a shaky laugh. 'I like. Probably won't last too long, though. It's been…a bit of a dry spell.'

Felicity didn't understand why that titbit of information should make her so happy, but it did. She liked the idea of being the one to break his drought.

He was breaking hers after all.

'Just a little taste.' She smiled as she reached for his belt buckle.

He dropped his hands and let her have her way. Triumph pulsed through her system, rich and heady, quickening her heartbeat and tingling at the juncture of her thighs.

Her hands trembled as she undid his belt then popped the button. She glanced at him as her fingers toyed with the zipper tab. He was watching her, his eyes hooded, his mouth full and brooding.

She couldn't wait to feel it on her again. Her mouth. Her neck. Her breasts.

Lower.

But for now it was her turn. Her mouth.

Felicity's pulse tripped as she slid the zip down and the fabric peeled back to reveal his impressive girth stretching the limits of his briefs. She looked up at him, her pulse skipping a beat to find him still watching her intently. Locking her gaze with his, she slid a hand up his thigh, inside his underwear and grasped the steely length of his erection.

He shut his eyes and groaned as she pulled it free. The sound was low and needy, sluicing over her like warm rain. His hand slid onto her shoulder and squeezed before his eyes drifted open again.

She made sure he was focusing on her before she transferred her attention to the solid weight of him in her palm and thanked whoever was the patron saint of trains for that strip of light at the bottom of the door allowing her a visual she was never going to forget.

He was big and hard and perfect. Thick and long. And for tonight—what was left of it—*hers*.

She leaned forward, placed her lips against the rigid perfection of him, kissing him there like he had first kissed her. Slowly and gently, testing things out, discovering his contours and the heady aroma of him, teasing him a little with her light kisses.

It wasn't until his quad started to tremble beneath her palm that she realised the level of control he was exercising. She glanced at him, seeing it in the taut planes of his face, feeling it in his grip on her shoulder. So she shut her eyes and let him have it all, leaning forward, pleasuring him with her mouth, taking him in as far as she could.

'Yes-s-s,' he hissed, sliding both hands into her hair. 'Yes.'

His gratification spurred her on and she went harder, revelling in the husky timbre of his breath and the utter hedonism of giving oral pleasure to a man she barely knew while she was topless in the privacy of a luxury train compartment.

She felt wild and reckless and completely wanton.

So freaking *James Bond*.

And she was never going to forget this night as long as she lived.

'Oh, God,' he groaned. 'We have to stop.'

But Felicity barely heard him. She was swept away in the moment, her pulse roaring through her ears.

It wasn't until he said, 'Stop,' again and pulled away that Felicity tuned back in.

'Sorry,' he panted. 'I'm too close...'

His forehead was scrunched, his lips tight. He looked in pain and completely undone, looming over her almost fully dressed, still potently aroused but somehow achingly vulnerable.

He didn't look like a man who was used to that state of being. His vulnerability hit her hard in the soft spongy spot that was never too far from the surface. She'd give him just about anything right now.

'What do you need?'

'To be in you.' He ducked down and kissed her hard. 'Now.'

The compartment tilted as the dizzying effects of the kiss continued even after it had finished.

Him in her? Now? *That* she could accommodate.

She shimmied back on the bed, dragging her yoga pants and underwear off in the process, aware of him watching the jiggle of her breasts with laserlike focus.

'Well?' she said as she wriggled to the centre of the bed, her nipples responding blatantly to his unashamed gaze. 'Am I the only one getting naked?'

'Nope.' He grinned, immediately toeing off his shoes and hauling his still-buttoned shirt over his head.

Watching him strip was sexy. Him *watching her* watch him strip even more so.

Felicity salivated at the perfection of his chest. It was wide at the shoulders, narrow at the waist. The muscles of his abdomen were defined but not excessively. Tanned and smooth, there was only a fine trail of hair trekking south from his belly button.

She wanted to kiss his chest. Smell it. Lick it. Stroke her fingers over the hills and valleys of his abs, trail them between his hips and watch how it turned him on. Feel the weight of it as he pressed her into the bed.

He stripped off his trousers and underwear together, revealing long, lean legs—more athletic than meaty. Before kicking them away he quickly retrieved his wallet from his back trouser pocket and plucked out a foil packet.

'Condom,' he said, as he took the two paces to her bed.

Felicity smiled as she let her gaze roam over every inch of his body. He was six feet plus of lean male animal and he was hers. 'Just the one?'

He put a knee on her mattress, tossing the packet near a pillow. 'We'll improvise.' He smiled.

And then he was lying on his side next to her, his head propped on his hand, his other hand trailing down her neck, through the valley between her breasts, down to her stomach, swirling around her belly button before continuing south all the way down through the soft curls of her pubic hair, stopping just before he reached ground zero.

Felicity's breath hitched as his finger hovered, taunting her. She doubted she'd last long either if he were actually to touch her.

She groped for the foil packet and thrust it at his chest. *His totally freaking awesome chest.* 'In me. Now. Remember?'

He smiled, his finger circling just out of reach. 'I can play a little first.'

She shook her head. 'It's been a while for me too.'

He regarded her for a moment before taking the condom and easing onto his back to roll it on. It was a position Felicity couldn't resist, taking advantage of his momentary distraction to move on top of him, straddling his hips, his fully sheathed erection sliding deliciously through the slick heat between her legs.

'God,' he muttered, his hands drifting up her belly to her breasts. 'You look magnificent.'

Felicity smiled as she arched her back and rubbed herself up and down the length of him. 'I feel pretty damn magnificent right now.'

His thumbs brushed her nipples and she shut her eyes, revelling in the heady glow of sexual abandonment for a moment or two.

But it just wasn't enough.

Her eyelids fluttered open to find him watching her again with an intensity that practically melted her into a puddle. She held his gaze as she leaned forward, tilting her pelvis and grasping his girth. His hands fell to her hips as she guided him to where she was slick and ready.

Where she *needed* him to be.

The feel of him there, so thick and *big*, was incredible. His eyes on her as she slowly sank down and he filled her—stretched her—was a whole different level. Felicity gasped as she settled flush against him, leaning forward with outstretched arms, bracing her hands on his shoulders, steadying herself as she took a breath.

'So good,' she muttered.

'God, *yes*,' he panted.

And it was. *So good.* Too good to just sit and do nothing. Too good not to move. Not to flex up and down and back and forth and round and round. Too good not to find a rhythm that was perfect and would drive them both towards a conclusion that had been building between them all night.

Her fingernails curled into his shoulders, his fingers gripped her hips like steel bands as they did just that, staring into each other's eyes as the tempo picked up, finding a rhythm and an angle that tripped her switch. His fingers slid between her legs again, not teasing this time but going straight to the spot she needed it most and rubbing sure and hard.

Nothing fancy. Just merciless pressure.

'God, yes,' Felicity gasped, drumming her feet behind her on the bed, riding him harder, faster as the fabric of her world started to tear from the inside out. Her thighs trembled, her nails dug in a little harder, her belly pulled taut.

Her orgasm hit hard roaring from a tiny quiver to an all-consuming pleasure storm within seconds.

'Yes,' he muttered, working her harder, faster, vaulting upright to press his lips to her neck, whispering, 'Yes, yes, yes,' as she slid her arms around his shoulders and came apart in his arms.

He flipped her on her back then, his forehead pressed into her neck, driving in faster and faster, sustaining her pleasure as he reached his own, groaning long and low into her ear as he came hard, sweat slicking the valley between his shoulder blades, his biceps trembling, her name on his lips as he spent himself inside her until he had no more to give and they both lay panting to the rock and sway of the train.

CHAPTER FOUR

CALLUM WAS EATING breakfast the next morning when Felicity finally put in an appearance. He'd left her sleeping two hours ago when the train had pulled into Broken Hill and woken him. It hadn't woken her and he'd told a hovering Donald not to wake her for the tour she'd been booked on or for breakfast.

'Of course,' he'd said, nodding his head. 'It was a late one, wasn't it?'

Callum's smile had been noncommittal. Little did Donald know just how late it had been. They'd enjoyed two more rounds of 'inventive' sex due to lack of protection. He'd only managed two hours' sleep.

But, then, insomnia had been part of his life for the last two years. He'd learned that lying around in bed, willing himself back to sleep, was counterproductive. Ignoring the tour options, he'd showered and gone through some more of his reading, as well as contacting his ride to let her know to delay her pick-up.

'Good morning,' Felicity said as she sat in the empty chair opposite him. Callum had been staring out the window, watching the scenery flash by, as he sipped his third cup of coffee. He had his sunglasses on to deal with the excessive sunlight flooding in through the glass because the view was too good to pass up.

He smiled at her. She looked fresh from the shower in jeans and a T-shirt, her wet hair pulled back into a ponytail low on her nape. An image of her riding him last night, honey-blonde strands flying loose around her bare shoulders, slid into his mind unbidden.

'It is,' he agreed. 'A very good morning.'

A small smile touched her mouth before a blush stole across her cheekbones and she dropped her gaze to the tablecloth briefly before raising it again. 'You're kind of chipper for someone who didn't get a lot of sleep.'

Callum shrugged. 'Some things are worth losing sleep over.'

'Absolutely.' She looked like she was about to say more but one of the wait staff interrupted, filling Felicity's cup with coffee. 'About last night...' she said after they departed, spooning in some sugar and stirring absently.

She seemed wary and unsure suddenly, staring at the circling spoon, reluctant to meet his gaze. Alarm bells rang in his head and his hair prickled at his nape. Was she going to suggest that they make it something more? Was she going to ask for his number? Or a date? Was she going to morph into some kind of clingy, bunny-boiler who wanted some kind of relationship?

Because, as incredible as it had been—and it had been *incredible*—he just didn't have time and space in his life at the moment for a romantic entanglement. He was trying to get his life back on track and last night had purely been the inevitable end to a couple of hours of flirting and one massive adrenaline hit.

Hadn't it?

Hell. He didn't even know her last name.

'I don't...' She placed her spoon on the saucer and glanced at him. 'I don't usually do this kind of thing.'

Callum nodded. There wasn't one part of him that thought she did. 'Yeah. I got that.'

'Not that I think,' she hastened to add, 'there's anything wrong with *hooking up*. It's just not...me, you know? Well, of course you know because I'm totally screwing this up in a very unsophisticated way, *exactly* like I've never done this before, but look...I live in this small town where everybody knows everybody else and they're all in each other's business and all the guys my age there think of me as Flick so I don't often get the opportunity to...'

He waited for her to continue but she appeared to have run out of steam. Callum couldn't figure out where she was going with this. Was the reason she was telling him she was a small-town girl her way of saying her daddy had a gun and he was now part of the family whether he liked it or not?

'Oh, God, sorry.' She grimaced, covering her face with her hand before dropping it again and shaking her head. 'I'm babbling. I *swore* I wouldn't babble.'

Callum laughed, which surprised the hell out of him. She really was quite cute when she was flummoxed. 'It's fine, don't worry about it. I'm not judging you and there *were* extraordinary circumstances last night.'

'Sure.' She picked up her cup and sipped, her gaze zeroing in on his. 'But you and I both know we were heading to bed even before our adrenaline-induced recklessness.'

There was no point denying that one. In fact, he was damn certain they'd have done it more than three times had their flirting not been so catastrophically interrupted.

'You're very direct, aren't you?' He liked that.

She laughed. 'Usually yes. Although not so much right now. It's the nurse in me.' She glanced out the window for a beat or two before looking at him again. 'What I'm trying to say—*very inelegantly*—is that I hope you don't think...I mean *want* or expect even...that this is anything more than just last night. Just two strangers on a train, in a...bubble almost. Indulging in something spontaneous. I mean, I like you but...hell, I don't even know your last name or where you live or what kind of doctor you are or even if you're going on to Perth.'

Callum opened his mouth to tell her it was okay. He got it. He felt exactly the same way about what had happened between them. About spontaneity. About getting out of his head and just not being himself for a night. But she held up her hand to ward it off.

'No. Don't tell me. I don't want to know any of it either. I'd kind of like to keep this whole thing as a big, delicious secret. This…crazy thing I did once that'll make me smile whenever I think about it. Maybe…' she smiled '…scandalise my grandkids about it one day.'

Grandkids. Of course there'd be grandkids. And kids. With honey-blonde hair and grey eyes. She was young and, despite what she said about the guys in her town, he had no doubt someone would snap her up.

Whereas he couldn't even look that far ahead.

'So,' Callum said, forcing himself to lighten the mood, 'you just want to use me for my body and callously walk away? Pretend it never happened?'

She pulled her bottom lip between her teeth as she nodded and said, 'Yes.' She toyed with her spoon again. 'Does that make me a terrible person?'

Callum chuckled at the little frown knitting her brow. He'd never met a woman who was such a compelling mix of confidence and uncertainty. 'No,' he teased. 'Relax. It was one night. We barely know one another. I promise you haven't broken my heart and I'm not about to drop down on one knee and ask you to marry me. You are not a terrible person and we should absolutely go our own ways after this with a smile on our faces and *very* fond memories of our night.'

'Is that how you're going to remember it?' she asked, placing her elbow on the table and propping her chin on her fist. 'Fondly?'

She was teasing now and he liked it. '*Very* fondly.'

She grinned. 'Me too.'

'Good. Now…' he thrust the breakfast menu at her '…order your breakfast. You *must* be hungry.'

Her gaze dropped to the menu but he could still see the smile playing on her mouth as she muttered, *'Starving.'*

Felicity ate like the train was about to run out of food. She was absolutely famished from her vigorous night between the sheets. Callum laughed at how much she put away and the happy little bubble around her grew.

It continued when they moved to the lounge. Jock's heart attack was a hot topic with their fellow travellers and everyone was agog at how they'd saved Jock's life. They were so impressed they didn't seem to mind the fact that both she and Callum had lied to them about what they did.

Or at least they didn't call them on it anyway.

The day flew and before Felicity knew it the train was rolling through the outer suburbs of Adelaide, bringing her closer and closer to home. She was treating herself to a few days in the city first, though. The last week in October was a perfect time to do her Christmas shopping and also hit the beach before the full tilt of summer. There were no beaches in the Clare Valley. Vineyards and antique shops, amazing restaurants with gourmet offerings and dinky little tearooms for sure, but no beach.

It was back to work on Monday and the magical time she'd spent in Sydney with her best friend Luci and the train trip and last night would all soon be pushed to the side as she morphed back into Flick and her life revolved around work and small-town life.

So she was going to savour this for as long as she could.

Half an hour later the train had pulled up at the platform and she was saying goodbye to her fellow travellers and Donald as she disembarked. A part of her wanted to stay on for ever, stay in this bubble for ever with Callum. But it was neither real nor possible so she channelled Flick and let it go, stepping onto the platform.

'Well, I guess this is goodbye.'

Felicity took a calming breath as Callum's familiar sexy rumble washed over her. She turned to face him, struck again by how sexy he was as her gaze roamed over his face, trying to remember every detail.

She was curiously reluctant to say goodbye. What did she say to a man who'd given her a moment in time she was never going to forget? Who had made her body sing? Who had made her feel sexy and desired?

Thank you just didn't seem enough.

'Do you have someone picking you up or...?'

Maybe they could catch a lift together? Maybe if he was also in the city for a few days they could...?

'We could share a taxi if you like. Where are you heading?'

'Oh, no, it's fine,' he said. 'I have someone picking me up.'

Of course. It was better this way really. A clean break.

'In fact...' he looked past her shoulder '...I think that may be her.'

Her. A sick moment of dread punched Felicity in the gut. She hadn't even asked him if he was involved with someone. She'd just assumed...

'Dr Hollingsworth?'

Felicity blinked at another very familiar voice as Callum waved and said, 'Over here.' She turned to find Mrs Baker, the wife of Vickers Hill's police chief, heading in their direction.

What the...?

'Mrs B.?'

'Oh, Flick, darling.' She smiled and pulled her into a big bear hug. 'What a surprise! Oh, wait...did I get my wires crossed? Julia was supposed to come but one of the receptionists had to go home sick, which left them short-staffed so she was ringing around to find someone else. I left a message on her phone that I'd do it but maybe she didn't check it and had already arranged for you to do the pick-up?'

Felicity had absolutely no idea what the other woman was talking about. 'The pick-up?'

'Yes.' Mrs Baker nodded. 'For Dr Hollingsworth here.'

Dr Hollingsworth? Felicity glanced at Callum. *He* was Dr Hollingsworth? The new locum? The one who'd done the house swap with Luci?

'*You're* Dr Hollingsworth?'

He frowned, obviously confused now too. 'Yes.'

Oh, hell... *What had they done?*

'So you're not here to pick him up?' Mrs Baker asked, looking as perplexed as Felicity but oblivious to her inner turmoil.

'No.' She shook her head. 'We've been on the train together. I just didn't...' she glanced at Callum '...know it.'

'Oh, how delightful.' Mrs Baker beamed. 'What a coincidence.'

Hmm. *Delightful* wasn't the way Felicity would describe it. She'd slept with the locum? A man she was going to have to face every day for two months?

How could they pretend it had never happened now?

'So...you know one another?' Callum asked, frowning at both of them, obviously trying to put the pieces together.

'Oh, yes.' Mrs Baker nodded vigorously. 'Flick's one of the practice nurses at Dr Dawson's surgery, aren't you, dear?'

Felicity watched as realisation slowly dawned on Callum's face. 'Oh. Right.'

'Isn't that an amazing coincidence?' Mrs Baker repeated.

'Yes...amazing,' he murmured through lips that were so tight Felicity worried they might spontaneously split open. *Fabulous.*

The man looked like he wanted to disappear. Or, at the very least, hightail it out of town. Felicity didn't know whether to be sad, mad, insulted or to push him back on the damn train herself.

'Right, well...' Mrs Baker said, still oblivious to the thick air of *what-the-hell* between them. 'Did you want a lift back home too, dear? Only we really do have to hit the road. It's a good two-hour drive, more with the peak-hour traffic.'

'Oh, no, thank you,' Felicity said, dragging her gaze off the incredulity in Callum's green eyes. 'I'm staying on for a few days.' *Thank God!* 'I'm not back till Sunday.'

'Oh, that's nice. Doing some Christmas shopping or seeing some bloke you're not telling any of us about?' Mrs Baker nudged her arm playfully.

Hardly. Given the last bloke she'd *seen* was now a certi-fied disaster. She returned the older woman's good-natured teasing with a wan smile, changing the subject. 'Well, you're right, you'd better be off. Say hi to everyone and I'll see them all on Monday.'

She forced herself to look at Callum like he was just some guy she'd met on the train and not someone she'd torn up the sheets with in what had been, without a doubt, the most memorable—and now the most disastrous—time of her life.

'It was nice meeting you, Dr Hollingsworth,' she said, willing a smile to her lips. She wasn't entirely sure she'd managed it but she ploughed on. 'I look forward to work-ing with you over the next couple of months.'

About as much as shoving a rusty fork in her eye.

He nodded, his mouth set in the grim line she'd first seen back at Central Station in Sydney. God—had it only been yesterday?

'Yes,' he said. 'Can't wait.'

He looked like he could do with a rusty fork too.

And then, because there *was* actually someone watch-ing her, Mrs Baker was ushering him along and out of the station and she was staring at his back. His chinos encasing those long athletic legs, his T-shirt stretching over those big shoulders, his hair brushing his nape.

A back she'd seen naked. A back she was damn sure she'd scratched up a little at one stage. Felicity shut her eyes and allowed herself an internal groan. How was she going to work with him every day and not think about their night together?

Not remember the bunch of his muscles under her hands as he'd loomed over her, the smell of his cologne on his neck, the deep groan when he'd orgasmed—*three times*.

Not relive every moment in glorious Technicolor?

Not want a repeat performance?

CHAPTER FIVE

FELICITY ALWAYS ARRIVED at work at seven in the morning. The practice didn't open until eight but she liked to grab a cup of tea and set things up at a leisurely pace. She liked to go through each of the doctors' appointment books as well as her own to mentally prepare herself for the day.

This morning she was here at seven because she hadn't been able to sleep. She'd driven into town deliberately after dark yesterday so no one could just drop in for a chat. She'd spent three days in Adelaide, trying to figure out a strategy to deal with Callum, and she still wasn't any closer.

She wasn't worried that anyone would find out. She didn't think Callum would be indiscreet. He didn't look like the kiss and tell type.

But *she* knew. Her *body* knew.

She'd been okay with acting so wildly outside her usual character when it had been a one-off. And she'd been fine to walk away from it and get back to the life she knew, loved and understood. The place, the people, the work that defined her. But with him constantly reminding her of something sizzling and exciting?

Constantly derailing her contented life?

She didn't need that kind of disquiet. She'd been lucky. She'd already had her big love. She didn't need some crazy, hot thing with a guy who was here for two months making her question all she held dear.

And even if she'd been actively looking for a man—which she wasn't—Callum did not fit the bill. She was only interested in long-term prospects and she was perfectly happy to wait. For it to happen when it happened. *If* it happened.

There wasn't any rush despite what every woman of a certain age in Vickers Hill thought.

The kettle boiled and Felicity shook herself out of her reverie. She was getting way ahead of herself. Catastrophising as usual. Also being a little egotistical. *Like she was so freaking irresistible.* Just because the man had ravished her in bed all night didn't mean he wanted anything more from her or that he wanted to carry on while he was here.

She was making way too much of it. It was two months, for Pete's sake. She could do *anything* for two months. They'd talk, set some rules and then she'd be cool, calm and collected. Polite. Professional. Friendly even. Vickers Hill was a great place to live in the middle of a famous wine region—she could play tour guide.

Felicity heard the back door open and glanced at her watch. She frowned. Dr Dawson was early today, he didn't usually arrive until seven thirty sometimes. Now he was cutting back his hours a little on his countdown to retirement he left it as late as a quarter to eight.

Felicity had worked for Luci's father for four years and would be grateful to him for ever for employing her when she'd fled back to Vickers Hill, licking her wounds post-Ned.

She turned to greet him, a smile on her face, knowing he'd come straight to the staffroom for a cuppa. But it wasn't Dr Dawson. It was Callum standing in the doorway, all long legs and wide shoulders, looking devastating in a dark suit and patterned tie.

Her stomach dropped. Her fingers tightened around her mug. She swore muscles between her legs tightened in some kind of Pavlovian response as heat coursed to all the erogenous zones he'd taken his sweet time getting to know.

So much for being cool, calm and collected. If her body was any hotter she'd be smoking. 'Oh. Hi.'

He nodded, his gaze guarded, reminding her of the brooding guy in the café that day. 'Hi.'

Awkward.

But, then, she'd always known it was going to be.

'You're early,' she said, to sever the stretching silence. 'You know you don't start till one each day, right?'

She knew he'd been in a couple of times already, orientating himself to the practice, because she'd been talking to Luci, who'd rung to tell her that Callum's brother Seb had turned up on her doorstep in Sydney and he was now *living* with her, but had also mentioned Callum dropping in to see her father and introduce himself to everyone.

He shrugged. 'Thought I'd get settled in.' He walked into the room and set the small plastic crate he was holding on the dining table. 'I also wanted to go over the clinic charts for this week. You know...' he gave a half-smile but it was strained and tight '...be prepared.'

Felicity nodded stiffly. Oh, yeah, he was a regular Boy Scout.

In any other person, she would have been impressed by the diligence but she'd thought she'd have more time to get her game face on this morning so she wasn't feeling terribly charitable.

'You'll have access to the appointment calendar on your computer in your office,' she said. 'I'll send you an invite to join but I'll just grab the printout now.'

It was her chance to temporarily escape and get herself together. He didn't try to stop her and for the thirty seconds it took her to snatch the list of today's appointments off the reception desk she was grateful.

She needed a breather. To hit the reset button.

She stared down at the list, not really seeing it. The Dawson general practice was one of two in Vickers Hill. There were two GPs. Bill Dawson was the original and had founded the practice almost forty years ago. About twenty years later he'd taken on a partner—Angela Runcorn—because the work had been too much for one and he'd wanted to have a woman for his female patients to have a choice. He and Angela each owned fifty percent of the practice.

Four years ago, and this was why Felicity had been employed, he'd taken on a part-time GP—Meera Setu. Meera and Felicity ran the afternoon specialty clinics together, which freed up a lot of appointment time. Monday was ortho clinic, Tuesday was diabetic, Wednesday was babies and Friday was immunisation. There was no clinic on Thursdays as it was Felicity's day for home visits.

But, with Meera going on maternity leave last week for two months, Dr Dawson had needed a replacement and had advertised for a locum. Given that it was for such a short amount of time, Felicity hadn't paid much heed to the process other than encouraging Luci to go to Sydney to do her course and pushing her to do the house swap with Callum when the possibility had been floated.

Except she'd only heard him being referred to as Dr Hollingsworth. And she'd never bothered to find out Callum's last name when she'd been getting naked with him between her sheets.

She made a mental note to always find out a guy's full name before doing the wild thing. Because now she'd be working closely with Dr Wild Thing *every* day.

Like right-hand woman close. And it all could have been avoided had she stopped to find out the basics—like his name!

'Here it is,' she said, injecting a lightness into her tone as she re-entered the staffroom.

He was at the sink, spooning coffee into a mug. She placed the list on the table next to the crate because there was no way she was getting any closer to him when she didn't have to.

'Thanks,' he said, picking up his mug and leaning his butt against the counter, his feet casually crossed at the ankles, which pulled the fabric of his trousers tight across his thighs.

'I'll forward you the email folder with all their electronic charts in a bit.'

'Thank you.' The silence built again. 'I checked up on Jock. They transferred him to hospital in Sydney and put in several stents. He's doing okay.'

Felicity nodded. 'Yes. Thanks. I spoke with the hospital this morning.'

Thankfully a noise in the hallway outside alerted her to someone else arriving and Felicity almost kissed Dr Dawson as he sauntered into the staffroom, his usual chipper self.

'Ah, Flick.' He smiled as he embraced her in a warm hug that smelled of the starch Julia, Luci's mum, always ironed his shirts with. 'Good to have you back. We almost fell apart without you.'

Felicity laughed, ignoring Callum in her peripheral vision. 'I'm sure Courtney caught on pretty quickly.'

Dr Dawson chuckled in that way of his that made other people want to join in as he pulled out of the hug. 'Now, then, I see you've met Cal. I think you two are going to get along famously.'

Felicity smiled at her boss then nodded in Callum's general direction. 'Yes. Callum and I have met.' She couldn't bring herself to call him Cal—he'd always be Callum to her.

'Oh, call him Cal,' Dr Dawson said. 'That's right, isn't it, son?'

At almost seventy Bill called every male under forty 'son'. It was his term of endearment.

'Cal's fine,' Callum said, ambling over to the table and sitting down. 'Most people call me Cal.'

Dr Dawson nodded, looking pleased with himself. 'You're bright and early. If you're trying to impress me, it's working.'

'Thought I'd look at the clinic appointments for the week. Familiarise myself with some charts.'

'Jolly good idea.' Dr Dawson nodded. 'Must do the same myself. Better get to it. Monday morning is always a madhouse here. I'll just make myself a cuppa and do the same thing.'

'I'll make it and bring it in for you, Dr Dawson,' Felicity offered.

She loved Bill Dawson almost as much as she loved her own father but he made an unholy mess in the kitchen and, like a lot of men, seemed completely blind to it. Also, Callum was a little too close for comfort now.

'Oh, no, Flick. Julia would rouse on me if I made the nurses get me a cup of tea.'

Felicity smiled. She knew that was the truth. Julia Dawson had been a nurse for over twenty years before Luci, her change-of-life surprise package, had come along. She'd worked part time on Reception for many years at the practice once Luci had gone to school and still helped out when things got hectic.

There was no greater advocate for the practice nurses than Bill's wife.

'I'm offering,' Felicity said, shooing him away from the sink as she approached. 'It'll be our little secret, I promise.'

Dr Dawson capitulated easily. 'Thank you.' He grinned. 'I'll see you later, Cal,' he said, moving towards the door. 'Don't hesitate to ask if you have any questions. Pop your head in or ask Angela or even our girl Flick. She knows more than all of us put together.'

Felicity kept her back turned, fiddling with the mugs as she snorted self-deprecatingly, which produced more chuckles from Dr Dawson as he exited.

She was excruciatingly conscious of Callum's gaze burning into her back as she made two cups of tea. When she was done she picked them up and finally turned to face him. It was disconcerting to find him still watching her, his brow crinkled, his mouth set in a brooding line.

'I used to be a Cal,' he said. 'Felt like one too. The life

of the party. The centre of the world. The man of the moment. I used to be like that.'

Felicity wasn't sure what this was about. Was he annoyed all these days later that she'd told him he didn't look like a Cal? Because he didn't—not to her mind. *Especially not now.* Or was he trying to explain why he hadn't introduced himself as Cal right out of the blocks?

Or did he just miss that Cal guy and want to reminisce? She had to admit to being curious about him herself.

It was hard to figure out what he meant. He was so tense and shuttered, so hard to read. 'What happened?'

He shrugged, looking down into his mug. 'Life. Stuff.'

She nodded. She didn't know what he wanted her to say. Did he want her to push or leave it alone? Something had obviously happened to Callum to change him.

Was that why he was here? In the middle of freaking nowhere? Fourteen hundred kilometres from his amazing harbourside apartment that Luci had raved about?

'You're a long way from home,' she murmured.

'Yeah.'

Felicity almost gave up. It was like pulling teeth. But she'd always been stubborn. 'Because you wanted to trade water for wine? Or…because you're running away?'

He glanced up from his mug, piercing her with his eyes. Running away it was.

Best she remember that.

'Because I'm newly trained and thought some rural experience would be good.'

It was a sound reason. Most GPs who locumed in rural areas and weren't from rural areas did so for the experience. Somehow, though, she didn't think that's what was going on here.

But whatever. It wasn't any of her business.

'Right. Well…' She looked at the mugs in her hand. 'I better deliver this, we open in fifteen minutes. I'll email you those files in a bit. Have you been set up on the computer?'

'Yes.' He nodded. 'Thanks.'

Felicity gave him a weak smile as she headed towards the door. 'No worries. Just yell if you need anything.'

But she hoped like hell he didn't.

It was almost three hours later before Felicity got around to emailing the file, although she had managed to send the appointment calendar invite through to Callum before things had got too crazy.

In the mornings Felicity was a general dogsbody. From receptionist to nursing duties, she was a jack of all trades and Mondays were always busy. It was like medical conditions multiplied over the two-day break. Plus there was a new doctor starting so that always brought out the rubber-neckers hoping for a glimpse.

Not that anybody had seen Callum yet, he was keeping his door firmly closed. A fact that didn't deter the Vickers Hill grapevine. They didn't need a sighting today. It was already in full swing because Mrs Mancini had spied him at the local supermarket, buying groceries at the weekend, and had declared him a bit of a catch.

She was surprised Mrs Mancini hadn't arrived with her gorgeous granddaughter who was a teacher at the local public school and who she'd been trying to marry off for the last two years. Three patients had already arrived bearing gifts of food for him.

Felicity picked up the plate of shortbread Mrs Robbins had brought with her. Her shortbread won the blue ribbon at the district fête every year and had been known to make grown men weep.

She took it with her to Callum's office. As far as she knew, he hadn't surfaced all morning and it was for him after all. She wanted to check he'd received the file and needed to get in there to set up for the orthopaedic clinic that started at one. There were three lots of plaster due to come off today and the plaster saw wasn't in the treatment room so it was probably in his office somewhere.

Also they needed to talk. Before the clinic. There were things to say. Although she wasn't sure how to start.

That's where the shortbread came in. If it all went badly, at least she could console herself with sugar.

She knocked on the door and opened it when she heard a muffled, 'Come in.'

Even dulled, his voice did wicked things to her pulse.

Damn. She was in trouble if his voice could make her legs weak through a closed door.

'Hey,' she said as she opened the door and shut it behind her then walked towards him all businesslike, concentrating on the plate of shortbread. 'I come bearing gifts.'

She glanced at him as she drew level with his desk and was pleased she was close enough to a chair should she collapse into it. *Glasses.* He was wearing glasses. Sexy glasses. The kind of trendy, designer wireless frames that hunky male models wore in advertisements for optometrists.

She wouldn't have thought he could look any sexier. *She'd seen him naked, for crying out loud.* But she'd been wrong. Callum with glasses was a whole other level.

'You wear glasses?'

It was possibly the dumbest thing she'd ever said. She might as well have said she'd carried a watermelon.

He peered at her over the top of those glasses. 'So do you.'

'Oh...yes.' She absently touched the frames she'd pushed to the top of her head. 'Just for reading and computer work.'

'Same here.' He took them off and tossed them on his desk and Felicity wished he'd put them on again.

He stared at her, obviously waiting for her to say something. 'Did you want something?' he asked, looking pointedly at the plate of shortbread.

His tone was brisk. Not unfriendly but businesslike. It

appeared she wasn't going to have to worry about any lines they'd crossed. He'd obviously retreated as far as he could.

It was just the bucket of cold water she needed.

'I came to check you'd received the file I sent you and to bring you these. Mrs Robbins made them for the new doctor. They're the best in the district. You also have a jar of Mrs Randall's rosella jam and Cindy Wetherall has made you a mulberry pie.'

He blinked. 'But…why?'

The incredulity in his voice would have been comical had it not been utterly genuine. Felicity shrugged. 'It's the country. That's how we welcome newcomers. Also there's a rumour going around town that the new doc is hot so you've gone to the top of the eligible list.'

'Eligible?'

'Yes, you know. Marriage, babies, the whole enchilada. We don't get a lot of new blood around here.'

His face morphed from mystified to horrified, which was another salient warning. He looked like two rusty forks would be welcome about now.

Obviously marriage and babies were not on his agenda. Or not in Vickers Hills anyway.

'What did you think you were going to get when you traded the city for the country?'

If her voice was a little on the tart side she didn't care. Honestly…for someone who'd come across as intelligent and articulate on the train, he was being rather obtuse.

'Not this.'

'Well…you'd better get used to it.' She plonked the plate of biscuits down. 'You're going to be well fed around here.'

He looked at them like they were a bomb that could possibly detonate at any moment. *Oh, for Pete's sake…* She had the strange urge to pelt him with one.

'Anyway… Did you get the files?'

He put his glasses back on and her pulse gave a funny little skip despite her annoyance. He looked at his computer screen. 'Thanks, yes. I've figured out the system and I've been reviewing all the charts for the week.'

He was being thorough. That was good. Being prepared and focused. Doing his homework.

But she still wanted to pelt him with shortbread.

'It looks pretty light,' he said, his eyes still glued to the screen. 'I'd see double the amount of patients in an afternoon in Sydney.'

There was no criticism in his voice. He was being matter-of-fact but it irked Felicity. She bit her tongue against the urge to tell him he could turn right around and go back to his precious Sydney.

It appeared their *talk* wasn't going to be necessary. It was obvious he didn't want to be here. She'd been worrying about nothing.

'Trust me, it'll take us all afternoon.'

'Okay. The clinic usually starts on time?'

'Yes. There are no appointments between twelve and one so we can have lunch then afternoon clinics start at one on the dot.'

'That's very civilised.'

Felicity gritted her teeth. Again, his tone wasn't critical but anger stirred in her chest anyway.

She supposed they didn't get time for lunch in Sydney.

'Well, you know what they say, the family that eats together stays together.'

He glanced at her. 'And you're all family here.'

Why did he make that sound like they were some kind of cult? 'Well...yes.' Where the hell was the charming guy from the train? The one she'd slept with?

Talk about a Jekyll and Hyde!

He nodded as if he was absorbing her answer before returning his attention to the screen. Felicity had to stop herself from rolling her eyes. 'Do me a favour? Have a look around here for the plaster saw when you're done with the charts?'

She'd planned on looking for it herself but frankly she didn't want to be around him any longer than she had to be. And she didn't need the temptation of a plaster saw in her hand when she felt like causing him physical harm.

'Sure,' he murmured, still focused on his computer.

Felicity wasn't sure if that was his way of dismissing her or not but she took her leave anyway.

She had no idea if he noticed.

CHAPTER SIX

CALLUM GLANCED UP as the door clicked shut. He hadn't realised Felicity had slipped out. He sighed and threw his glasses on the desk again, massaging the bridge of his nose with two fingers.

Damn it. He'd been too short with her. He hadn't meant to be, she'd just caught him at a bad moment. He'd been trying to concentrate on his work, to push away the powerful feelings of regret that were threatening to swamp him, but sitting here at his desk in a Vickers Hill general practice he couldn't deny them any longer and she'd arrived in the middle of his pity party.

He was a GP. A general practitioner. The last two years he'd been in training for this so it hadn't seemed quite real. But now he was here, in his first GP job, and it was as real as it got.

Goodbye, hot-shot surgeon. No more triple As, carotid endarterectomies or vascular bypasses. His life now revolved around tonsillitis, hypertension, reflux and asthma. No more international surgical conferences or pioneering new techniques or glitzy dinner parties. No more cut and thrust of the operating theatre. It was all rosella jam and mulberry pie...

So not the way he'd pictured his life turning out.

Sure, after this he was heading back to the prestigious north shore practice where he'd undergone a lot of his training. He'd never been given home-made anything by any of the patients there but it wasn't scrubs and the smell of the diathermy either.

Still, none of it was Felicity's fault and they had to work

together so he needed to get his head out of his rear end. He hadn't been prepared for the leap in his pulse when he'd seen her again this morning. He'd spent the last few days trying to compartmentalise her in his head as the woman on the train. A fantasy. A very sexy, very real fantasy that he thanked his lucky stars for but a fantasy nonetheless.

He'd thought he'd succeeded.

And then she'd been in the staffroom and his libido had growled back to life again as a rush of memories from the train had filled his head.

She hadn't looked like the woman in the fringed boots or the little black dress. She'd been in her uniform—a pair of loose-fitting blue trousers and a polo shirt with 'Dawson Family Practice' embroidered across the pocket. The shirt was also loose and her honey-coloured hair was tied back in a low ponytail at her nape.

But she *had* looked like the woman in the yoga pants and bare feet who'd shared her bed with him and damn if that hadn't made him all fired up. And messed with his head. Why else would he have babbled on about being a Cal?

Oh, God. He'd been inept...

But it had seemed vital suddenly that she know. To make her understand that he had been a different person once. That he *was* capable, even if that guy felt lost to him for ever.

To not judge him as the man she saw now.

Which hopefully she wouldn't because that guy had just acted like an insensitive jerk.

He'd come here to get away from the tentacles of his past. To begin his new career away from judging eyes. To get some clear air before he went back to a world that was used to seeing him as an entirely different person.

To be happy, goddamn it.

Or at least less miserable.

He just hadn't realised how hard it was going to be. He'd put too much expectation on this first day. That starting it would be some miracle cure. Some invisible line in the sand that held magical powers of career satisfaction by just stepping over it when clearly it was going to take time. He was going to have to get used to it. To the change in pace and clientele and his core duties. To take one day at a time and have faith that each day would be better than the last.

It was that or become a bitter old man. And he refused to let that damn cricket ball win.

The clinic started promptly but didn't go according to what Felicity, or the patients, were used to. Callum was efficient in the extreme. No wonder he had queried the appointment numbers when he seemed to have mentally allotted five minutes to each one and zipped through the list like he was trying to set a new world record.

Usually, with Meera, each appointment would last between ten and fifteen minutes. But Callum didn't believe in pleasantries. He wasn't rude. He was polite and respectful but he didn't dillydally either, didn't open himself to chitchat, preferring to cut straight to the chase. Review the problem. Make a diagnosis. Order a test, an X-ray, a pill or dish out some medical advice.

Thank you for coming. *Next!*

Some city practice was going to lap him up with his billing rate. But that's not what they were about at the Dawson Family Practice and by the time they'd worked their way through to their second-last patient—at *four o'clock*—Felicity was cranky. The clinics always ran until at least five and usually closer to six.

She had no doubt Callum looked on it as efficiency. There were more people in the cities, therefore more demand on GP services. Double- and triple-booking were common practice. But he could keep it as far as she was concerned. Her patients deserved more than a paint-by-numbers doctor.

Old Mr Dunnich came in, bearing a bunch of roses. He was a big old wizened bloke in his mid-eighties, used to stand six-four and didn't have the belly he was sporting now in his grape-growing days.

'These are for you, Doc,' he said in his slow country drawl. 'Don't usually go around giving flowers to blokes but the wife insisted.'

Callum seemed as puzzled by the gesture as Mr Dunnich. 'Oh…thanks,' he said, taking them awkwardly and putting them on his desk before ploughing on. 'Now, let's have a look at those bunions, shall we?'

Mr Dunnich shot her a perplexed look. In fact, she knew him well enough to see a fleeting flash of offence. Mr Dunnich's prize roses were a thing of beauty, and the perfume floated to Felicity from across the other side of the room within seconds. There wasn't a person alive—including clueless men—who didn't comment on how spectacular they were.

Felicity wasn't usually a person who harboured murderous intent but she had to suppress the urge to hit Callum across the head with the nearest heavy object, which just happened to be a tendon hammer.

It *probably* wouldn't kill him should she be unable to suppress the urge to use it.

Mr Dunnich took off his shoes and socks in silence. Normally he was always up for a chat. He could talk about his roses all day and what the man didn't know about growing grapes for wine wasn't worth knowing. But he did what all old men from the country did when feeling socially awkward—he clammed up.

Callum examined both big toes. The silence stretched, which was obviously making Mr Dunnich uncomfortable enough to try and initiate some conversation. 'The pain's getting worse, Doc, but I really don't want to have to go under the knife. I don't want to leave Lizzy alone.'

'I see,' Callum said, poking and prodding as he asked a few questions. 'Okay,' he said briskly a moment or two later. 'You can put your shoes back on.'

Mr Dunnich did as he was told. 'I'm going to try you on this new medication,' Callum said, turning to his computer and using the electronic prescription system to generate a script to give to the chemist. The printer spat it out and he handed it over. 'It's had good results for arthritic pain. One twice a day for a week then come back and see us at the clinic next week and we'll reassess.'

'Rightio,' Mr Dunnich said, taking the printout and glancing at her, obviously not sure if the consult was over. He hadn't been in and out in five minutes ever.

Felicity smiled at him encouragingly, her heart going out to him. 'I'll see you out, Mr Dunnich.'

Again, Callum hadn't been rude but he hadn't been welcoming either. He'd been brisk and efficient and oblivious to his patient's awkwardness.

'I need to find a vase for these anyway,' she said, ignoring Callum as she swooped up the roses. She buried her face in them as she caught up to the patient and linked her arm through his. 'They're gorgeous, aren't they? What are these ones called?'

The old man's wrinkled hand landed on hers as he gave her a couple of pats. 'I struck this one myself.'

Felicity was back with the roses in a vase in under a minute. She put them on his desk, desperately hoping he was allergic to them, but he didn't shift his attention from the computer, squinting at it instead as he clicked around different views to assess the X-ray on the screen.

'This radius looks good,' he declared, finally looking at her over the tops of his glasses, and it hit her again how they loaned him that extra dollop of sexy.

It wasn't a thought she welcomed. How could she have the hots for someone who didn't have a clue about connecting with his patients? Who she wasn't even sure she *liked* any more.

Because you've seen the other side...

Felicity hated it when the voice in her head was right. She

had seen a very different side to Callum. One who had been competent and *compassionate* as well as chatty and flirty.

She'd liked that guy. *A lot.*

And compassion was always going to trump competence and looking great in glasses.

'It's healed very nicely.' His gaze returned to the screen. 'Can you take the plaster off then send her in to me?'

Aye, aye, sir. 'Certainly, Dr Hollingsworth.'

He looked up abruptly, a frown between his brows. 'You don't have to call me that,' he said. 'Callum is fine.'

Felicity figured 'jerk' was even better but she wisely held her tongue.

'Looks like we're going to both get an early mark,' he said, glancing at his watch, clearly pleased with himself.

Felicity's blood pressure shot up a notch or two. She didn't want a damn early mark. She wanted her patients to feel like they were more than a body part or some medical problem to cure or treat.

'I'll just see to Pauline.'

Felicity hit the waiting area with a full head of steam and a bunch of uncharitable thoughts. 'Hey, Pauline, you can come through now,' she said, forcing herself to smile so she wouldn't scare any of the waiting patients.

Pauline had slipped on the wet tiles around her pool and put her arm out to break her fall, snapping her radius instead. She was a few years older than Felicity but with three little kids she was a regular at the practice.

Felicity led her into the treatment room and Pauline sat on the central table over which hung a large, adjustable operating theatre light. It could be moved higher and lower and angled any which way required when suturing or other minor procedures were performed.

'You ready for this?' Felicity asked as she applied her face mask, grateful for her glasses being a little more glamorous eye protection than the ugly, clunky plastic goggles that the practice supplied. Cutting through plaster kicked up a lot of dust and fibres.

'I am so ready for this, Flick. Those kids of mine have sensed I'm weak and have been running riot these last six weeks. I can't wait to show them Mummy's back.'

Felicity laughed. 'All righty, then. It looks scary and it's going to be loud, okay?'

She turned it on to demonstrate. The oscillating saw with its round blade whined as loudly as any handyman's saw. She turned it off. 'The blade vibrates, it doesn't cut. If it comes into contact with your skin it can't hurt you. But it won't, I promise. Once I get down to the last layer I'll switch to plaster spreaders and some kick-arse scissors.'

'Yep. Cool.' Pauline nodded vigorously. 'Let's do it.'

It took fifteen minutes to remove the cast. Using the loud saw was actually quite therapeutic. By the time she'd sent Pauline on her way to Callum, Felicity wasn't feeling anywhere near as annoyed as she had been.

She did, however, get some dust or fibre in her right eye, which became more and more irritating as she cleaned up the treatment room. She ambled over to the mirror hanging behind the door to see if there was anything obvious. Her eye was red from her rubbing it but there was nothing apparent in it.

Damn. She'd get a lecture from Bill for sure about wearing the correct safety equipment and she'd only have herself to blame. She'd always considered her own glasses as good eye protection—for plaster removal anyway—and now she was going to have to revise that opinion.

The irritation grew worse and out of desperation she grabbed a handful of plastic saline ampoules, twisted off their tops and moved to the sink. She leaned her head over and turned it on the side, her right eye down and bent her knees to bring her closer to the porcelain so she wouldn't make a mess.

It was an awkward position but at least the saline ran

straight into the sink as she gently trickled ampoule after ampoule into her eye.

'What on earth are you doing?'

Felicity's pulse leapt both at the unexpected interruption and who it belonged to. Not exactly the most elegant position to be found in, especially as she already felt like an idiot for being in this situation. Her earlier crankiness returned. 'What does it look like?'

'You got something in your eye?' His voice grew nearer and she could see him approach in her peripheral vision, coming to a halt, his hands on his hips as he watched her, her eyes about level with his fly.

She tried valiantly not to go back to that night again but failed.

'Give the man a cigar.'

'Is this from removing the plaster?'

'Yes.'

He held out his hand for the remaining ampoules. 'Let me help.'

'I'm fine. You've got your early mark, go home.'

She may have liquid in one eye and a side view from the other but she didn't need to see his glare—she felt it all the way down to her toes.

'Are you angry at me for some reason? Do you have something against efficiency? Or is this some self-loathing guilt trip of yours because of what happened on the train, which is suddenly now wrong and somehow my fault? Because if we've got a problem then I really wish you'd just come out and say it.'

Felicity glared right back, which was difficult considering what she was doing. Yes, she was angry but it had absolutely nothing to do with the train or any kind of guilt trip. Hindsight was always twenty-twenty but she could never hate herself over that night.

This was purely about today. Unfortunately it wasn't her place to chastise the new doctor about the way he practised. Or any doctor for that matter. There were protocols and formal procedures in place for those kinds of things.

Not that she'd ever had any cause.

If Dr Dawson asked her how Callum was going she'd say he was diligent and efficient. But if there were complaints from the patients, he was on his own.

'No problem,' she muttered. She could bite her tongue over this. She *would*. If it killed her. Because she'd be damned if she did a single thing to make him think she was playing some petulant game because she was embarrassed about what had happened between them.

'Good. Now let me look at your damn eye and see if there's anything obvious.'

'I already looked. Couldn't see anything.'

He folded his arms. 'So let me check now you've treated it.'

Felicity realised her recalcitrance wasn't doing her any favours. She could act like a two-year-old or take advantage of the professional help being offered like an adult. 'Fine,' she muttered, reaching for the paper towel dispenser nearby. He beat her to it, pulling off two sheets and passing them over as she righted herself.

'Thank you.' She injected a more conciliatory note into her voice as she dabbed at her wet face. He was offering to help. It wasn't his fault she was in this situation.

'Over here,' he said, moving to the centre of the room near the examination bed. He glanced at the overhead light. 'Where's the switch for this thing?'

Felicity tossed the paper towel on the bed and went up on tippy toes to reach one of the vertical handles. She pulled it down and located the switch. Light pooled around them. He squinted and moved so the back of his head blocked the light. The halo affect was disconcerting considering she'd been thinking of him as the devil incarnate most of the day.

'Okay,' he said, sliding his hands either side of her face. 'Let me look.'

The sizzle from his contact was also disconcerting. They were standing close. Too close. Her brain rejected the nearness while her body flowered beneath it. He wore the same aftershave as he had on the train and if she shut her eyes she could almost imagine them being gently rocked.

Felicity tried to pull away but he held on tight. 'It's better, much less gritty.'

He set his thumbs beneath her jaw and used them to angle her head. 'That's good,' he murmured, obviously ignoring her as he peered into her eyes. Or her *eye* anyway. Her pulse hammered madly at every pulse point, surely he could feel it beneath the pads of his thumbs?

He instructed her to look up then down then to both sides, which she did eagerly. Frankly she was pleased to look anywhere but right at his big handsome face in those beyond-sexy glasses. Being up this close and personal to Callum was a seriously crazy temptation.

It was madness and she reached for something to evoke a bit of sanity.

Think about Mr Dunnich.

But all she could think about was how good Callum smelled and she understood a little better why some women stayed with men who weren't good for them.

'Well...I can't see anything,' he announced.

The statement made her forget she was trying *not* to look at him as she did exactly that. *'Quelle surprise,'* she murmured, their gazes locking, his green one intense as his thumbs stroked along her jaw.

It was so damn good she swayed a little.

The sensible person inside her scrambled for a reason to pull away, for something, anything to break the spell he was weaving with the seductive stroke of those clever thumbs.

It was then that she noticed it.

'Your left pupil is misshapen.' There was an area where the black of the pupil appeared to have bled into the green of his iris. 'It's larger than the other one too.'

That did it. His hands slid off her face and he took a step back. Felicity reached for the table to steady herself as her body mourned his abrupt withdrawal.

'Yes.'

'Is that genetic or from an injury?'

The brooding line had returned to his mouth and for a moment she thought he wasn't going to answer her. 'An injury.'

She quirked an eyebrow. A rusty fork maybe? 'Are you going to make me guess?'

It wasn't any of her business but it didn't stop her being curious as hell. It was obvious from his reaction that it had been serious.

'A cricket ball.'

Felicity's wince was spontaneous and heartfelt. She almost grabbed her own eye in sympathy. 'Ouch.'

'Yeah…' His fingers fiddled with the sheet on the examination table. 'It was a bit of a mess.'

'Define mess.'

She expected him to dismiss her query and leave, and if she wasn't very much mistaken he looked tempted to do just that. But then he shrugged. 'Fractured zygoma. Blown globe. Hyphema. Partial retinal detachment.'

Her wince increased. 'Holy cow! Who was bowling to you? Mitchell Johnson?'

His lips twitched into the grimmest semblance of a smile she'd ever seen. 'One of my mates used to bowl for the under-nineteen Australian side. He's still got it.'

Maybe this was what Callum had been referring to this morning when he'd been going on about being a Cal once upon a time. He was just as tense and shuttered. 'Do you have a sight deficit?'

If anything, the line of his mouth grew grimmer. 'I only have seventy percent vision in my left eye, hence these.' He pointed at his glasses.

Seventy percent. This morning she'd been sure something had happened to Callum to change him—something big—and now she was absolutely convinced. Was the 'life' and 'stuff' he'd talked about the injury to his eye?

Had it turned Cal into a Callum?

Great. A wounded guy. Appealing to her soft underbelly. She was hopeless with them. *This* was the guy from the train, not the one she'd seen today, and she was finding it hard to reconcile the two.

'Is the mydriasis permanent?'

He grimaced. 'It's a work in progress. It's constricted quite a bit since the injury but the specialist thinks after all this time it's about as good as it'll get, and unfortunately I concur.'

'How long ago did it happen?'

'Two and a half years.'

Felicity did a quick calculation in her head. So the accident had happened six months before he'd commenced his GP training. It had probably taken that long for his eye to recover sufficiently to be useful.

Which begged the question, had it always been his plan to train to become a GP? Or had his injury caused him to change career path?

She had a feeling that was very much the case.

'So I take it being a GP hadn't been your grand plan?'

His lips twisted and his self-deprecating laugh was harsh, grating in the silence of the room. 'No.'

Felicity marvelled that such a little word could hold so much misery. This accident had obviously gutted him.

'What was your specialty before you did your GP training?'

He dropped his gaze to the sheet again. 'I was a surgeon.'

Ah. Well, now. His concentration on body parts and medical problems rather than the patient as an individual suddenly made sense. Felicity had spent some time in the operating theatres when she'd been training in Adelaide. She'd quickly come to realise she would never make a scrub nurse. Impersonalising patients and the lack of any real contact with them had driven her nutty.

She hadn't wanted to work in a place where patients were known by their operative site. The leg in Theatre Two, the appendix in Theatre Five or the transplant in Theatre Nine.

Patients had names and she liked to use them.

'What kind of surgeon?'

'Vascular.'

Felicity suppressed the urge to whistle. Impressive. She could see him all scrubbed up, making precise, efficient movements, working his way through his list, conscious of his next patient waiting. 'Did your sight issues interfere with that?'

'Oh, yes.' His tone was harsh with a bitter end note. 'My depth of field and visual acuity in the left eye were shot. A lot of the work I did was microsurgery and...' he glanced up, his gaze locking with hers '...I didn't trust myself.'

The emotions brimming in his eyes belied the hard set of his face and punched Felicity in the gut. 'But surely with time—'

His short, sharp laugh cut her off. 'They'll only give me a conditional driver's licence, they're not going to let me be in charge of a scalpel.' He shoved a hand through his hair, looked away, looked back again. 'It has improved, but not enough. Not to be a surgeon. I'm not prepared to take that kind of risk with somebody's life.'

And there was the compassion. Callum had obviously had the rug pulled right out from under him but he was a doctor first and foremost and doing no harm was the code they lived by.

It was honourable but obviously not easy. This was the man from the train. The one who had been great with Jock and Thelma and the other group of oldies. The one who had laughed and flirted with her. The one who had looked into her eyes in her compartment and *connected* with her.

She gazed at him, trying to convey her understanding. 'I'm sorry. That must have been very hard for you.'

And she *was* sorry. He may have annoyed her today but at least now she understood him a little better. Would maybe even cut him a little slack. He'd given up a lot. Having your hopes and dreams quashed wasn't easy. She knew that better than anyone.

He shook his head dismissively. 'It is what it is.'

She took a step towards him, put her hand on top of his. 'Yeah. Doesn't make it suck any less, does it?'

His gaze flicked to their hands before returning to her face and she caught a glimpse of a guy who was adrift before he shut it down and slid his hand away, tucking it in his pocket as he moved back a few paces.

'Anyway,' he said, his eyes not quite meeting hers, 'maybe take home some liquid tears to settle any residual irritation.'

Felicity didn't need him to tell her that but the way he was judging the distance to the door she figured it was just a segue to him leaving. The thought needled but she had no idea why.

'Yep, great, thanks for your help.' She turned and headed for the sink, flipping on the water and washing her hands because the other ninety-nine times today hadn't been enough.

But it gave her something to do and the opportunity for him to slip away, which he took with both hands.

CHAPTER SEVEN

CALLUM WAS LOOKING forward to the home visits even if Felicity had seemed less than impressed by his request to accompany her. She hadn't said no but she had queried the necessity of it. He felt it was essential to know about this important service, especially if he was ever going to be called out to one of the patients during his one weekend in three on-call days.

She hadn't had a comeback for that but her stony profile as she drove them to their first appointment spoke volumes.

He wasn't sure what was going on with her. Despite her protestations on Monday that they didn't have a problem and the obvious empathy in her eyes when he'd told her about the accident, the last couple of days had still been awkward.

Sure, she was polite and efficient. But he wouldn't exactly say she was knocking herself out to be friendly. Not like she was with her patients.

Not like she'd been that day on the train.

Was that where Felicity's awkwardness was springing from? The train? Did she regret what had happened? Did she resent that seeing him every day she couldn't put it away in some neat little box somewhere? Or was she worried that he'd kiss and tell and spoil her St Felicity reputation?

Because there was one thing he'd learned in his few short days at the practice—Felicity could do no wrong.

Everyone loved Felicity.

Their version of her anyway because she was a very different Felicity from the one he'd met on the train. Sure, she was as friendly and easygoing with the patients as she had been with their travelling companions, but here, in Vickers

Hill, she was very definitely *Flick*. The small-town girl, the friendly nurse, everyone's mate.

She knew who everyone was and who they were related to. She knew where everything was found, everything anyone had been treated for in the last four years and, it seemed, everyone's birthdays. As well as having practically every phone number in the town memorised.

She *was* a freaking saint.

And he'd gone and thoroughly debauched her.

He didn't think the town—aside from one or two busybodies—cared what their saint did in her private time but what if she thought they did? They hadn't talked about what had happened between them, not since discovering they would be working together, so maybe it was time they did.

He glanced at her profile. Her forehead was crinkled into a frown, her lips pursed. *Maybe not.* Safer to stick to work-related topics and hope she eventually relaxed when she realised he wasn't here to make her life difficult.

'So,' he said, his sunglasses in place as the harsh October sun cut through the glass of the windscreen, 'the purpose of the home visits is?'

'A federally funded initiative to keep older and less able patients in their homes and in the community and out of care.'

She parroted the facts as if he'd pushed a button on her somewhere that read *Press here for information.* She didn't shift her gaze off the road. Didn't glance at him for a second.

Callum ploughed on, bloody-minded now. 'What kind of things do you do when you're with a patient? Are there specific things or is it just a general social call?'

Her fingers wrapped, unwrapped and wrapped around the steering wheel again. 'A lot of different things. I deal with any specific medical issues of the day but mostly patients go into the practice if they have anything acute. I do blood-pressure and blood-sugar checks as well as full yearly health checks when they come due. I make sure their pre-scriptions and referrals are up to date. I do a lot of ordering.'

'Ordering?'

She at least nodded this time. 'Products. Medical sup-plies. Incontinence products, stoma bags, peritoneal dialy-sis supplies, test strips as well as equipment like feeding pumps, shower chairs or Zimmer frames.'

'Sounds busy.'

'It's not all tea and scones,' she said.

He could have cut the derision with a knife. He was about to call her on it when Felicity engaged her blinker and said, 'First cab off the rank is Mr Morley.'

Callum looked out the window to see an old-fashioned, low-set cottage that could do with some TLC. She undid her seat belt then looked at him for the first time since he'd sat in the car.

'These people know me. They trust me. They're often wary of strangers and prefer talking to a nurse about their issues over a doctor. They might be suspicious of you. Just try to…'

Callum thought she was going to say 'not screw it up' but she continued, 'Stay in the background, okay?'

She didn't give him time to reply, reaching for the handle and stepping out of the vehicle.

Her faith in him was heartening.

What followed was an intense five hours. Callum saw the gamut of small-town life all in one afternoon as St Felic-ity ministered to her flock. It wasn't the most efficient sys-tem he'd ever seen. Too much chatter and drinking of tea and eating of cake or whatever piece of home-made cook-ing was presented to them for his liking, but it appeared to be the ritual and with Felicity's advice ringing in his ears there was no way he was declining. He'd never eaten so well in his life.

He was going to have to do some serious working out when he got back to Sydney.

He followed Felicity's lead after earning her glare when he'd declined something at their second stop. It just wasn't done, apparently. And she was right, the patients were leery of him to start with so if eating food that was offered at all their dozen stops helped with the warming-up process then when in Rome...

That all changed when they got to their last call—Meryl's house. She didn't appear to have a last name or require any kind of formal address as Felicity's other patients had.

Just Meryl, apparently.

Her house was a small cottage with a deep bull-nosed veranda. Dreamcatchers and wind chimes of all types and sizes hung from the guttering. The pungent spice of incense prickled Callum's nose and a small shrine with a Buddha and a variety of candles and flowers was set up in one corner of the living room.

Meryl took to him right away. She was sitting in a big stuffed recliner and was possibly the most wrinkled person Callum had ever met. But there was a strength and agility to her movements that made him think she was probably younger than she appeared.

He stuck out his hand when Felicity introduced them. Her hand was soft but her grip was firm as she pulled him nearer, forcing him to lean in closer.

'Cal,' she murmured, immediately shortening his name in a husky voice that sounded like the product of a pack-a-day habit. She looked straight into his eyes, taking her time to study him. 'You have an unhappy aura,' she finally declared, releasing his hand.

Callum glanced at Felicity for an interpretation in case there was one other than the obvious—Meryl was a little nutty. She shot him the most faux innocent eyebrow-lift he'd ever seen in his life. He should have known that someone who lived in a house guarded by dream catchers was going to be a little...alternative.

'Meryl reads auras,' she said, a small smile playing on her lips.

That little knowing smile drew attention to her mouth and it was just about the sexiest damn thing he'd ever seen. All week he'd been trying not to think about that mouth and where she'd put it on his body. Her attitude towards him had helped. But now she was finally pulling the stick out of her butt it was impossible not to go there again.

Impossible not to want to familiarise himself with it again and kiss the smile right off that sexy mouth.

'Hmm, it's looking a little happier now,' Meryl mused.

Callum blinked at the running commentary on the state of his aura, pulling his gaze from Felicity's. He gave himself a mental shake. The last thing he wanted Meryl proclaiming was his aura's massive erection.

'Sit down here, Cal,' Meryl said, patting an old vinyl chair beside her.

Callum would rather sit outside in the car but there was no way he could get out of this without looking rude. The normal rules of doctoring just didn't apply in the community, certainly not in a house that could have belonged in Oz.

He glanced at Felicity, who was obviously finding the situation highly amusing.

'What colour's Felicity's aura?' he asked, turning to give all his attention to Meryl. Thankfully, Felicity was on his right so he could see her smile slowly deflating.

Although he was sure she had no cause to worry. The saintly Felicity's aura was no doubt rainbowesque and probably smelled like strawberries and candy canes.

'It'll be the same as usual,' Meryl said, flicking her gaze to Felicity. Callum was inordinately pleased when the older woman raised an eyebrow. 'Or maybe not... It's *usually* so balanced but it does look a little...ruffled today.'

Callum smiled as the tables were turned and Felicity

frowned and put a hand to her belly. Meryl's gaze cut back to him and he pressed his lips together so she couldn't see him gloating, although there was something all-seeing about Meryl that couldn't be easily dismissed.

Her eyes narrowed speculatively. 'You're staying at Luci's place, right?'

Callum nodded, feeling on solid ground with standard questioning. 'Yes. And she's staying at my place in Sydney.'

'And how long are you staying in Vickers Hill?'

'I'm here for eight weeks.'

'No.' Meryl shook her head slowly as her gaze darted all around his head before she peered into his eyes. It was more thorough than any of the dozens of specialists with their fancy high-powered microscopes had ever managed.

Frankly, it put an itch up his spine.

'You'll be here for much longer than that.'

Callum broke the eye contact with difficulty. No. *He was going back to Sydney.* To his harbourside apartment and his job that started in the New year. Vickers Hill was just a pit stop. A place for some clear air.

He glanced at Felicity, who wasn't looking so sure of herself now either. She appeared ready to deny it if he didn't.

'I can assure you,' Callum said, dredging up his most positive smile for Meryl. It wasn't one he'd used a lot these last two years and it didn't feel right on his face. 'I'm only here short term.'

Meryl just smiled and patted his hand. 'You'll see. It's okay,' she assured him. 'It'll work out. You were meant to come here. It's your destiny. It's in your aura.'

Callum didn't know what to say to that. Clearly Meryl wasn't about to change her mind and what did it matter what some crazy old lady on an incense high who read auras said?

He was in charge of his destiny.

'Right, well.' Felicity clapped her hands together. 'Let's get your blood pressure checked, Meryl.'

Callum vacated the seat, grateful to her for rescuing him

from any more talk of auras and destinies and staying in Vickers Hill.

He could have kissed her.

He *really* could have kissed her.

Callum was looking out the passenger window of Felicity's car when she rolled to a stop in front of Luci's house. He still wasn't used to living in a place that was so country kitsch. It was a turn-of-the-century stone cottage with a chimney and a wraparound porch along which grew a thick bushy passionfruit vine laden with fruit. The entire garden was beautifully manicured and a riot of colour that reflected the froufrou decor of the interior.

Lots of lace at the dinky little windows and white shabby chic furniture complemented the exposed oak ceiling beams and the oak kitchen tops. It was a far cry from his sleek, minimalist apartment dominated by huge unadorned windows from which to admire the stunning water view.

Callum glanced at Felicity, who was staring straight ahead at some point on the road. They hadn't talked at all from Meryl's to here. He figured they were both lost for words. 'So… Meryl…she's a little…colourful?'

Her head snapped around to glare at him. 'And what's wrong with that?' she demanded. 'We can't all be hip, cool Sydneysiders.'

Callum blinked at her unexpected vehemence, holding up his hands to indicate his surrender. Her chest rose and fell markedly. 'Hey,' he murmured. 'It wasn't a criticism.'

She glared at him for a beat or two before returning her attention to the road and huffing out, 'Sorry.'

Callum sighed. Okay. *Enough.* Enough of this. Something was obviously bothering her and he couldn't ignore it any longer, hoping she'd snap out of it. He was going to have to mention the elephant in the room.

Or the car, as it turned out.

'You don't have to worry about me saying anything to anyone about what happened between us.'

That earned him another short, sharp, slightly askance glance. 'I didn't for a minute think I had to.'

Callum raised both his eyebrows. Okay…so what was this all about? It couldn't be his work. He'd been his usual competent, efficient self. He may not be fully resigned to his new career but he knew he did good work. The same way he always knew he did good surgery.

He was a Hollingsworth—they always excelled at what they did.

'Okay. Well…sorry. It's just…you've been angry at me all week and I thought…I just needed to reassure you, that's all. If that's what you're worried about.' He thought maybe, deep down, she was, she just didn't want to acknowledge it so it was worth saying again. 'I don't kiss and tell and what happened that night is between us only.'

'Good.' She glanced away, fixing her gaze on the steering wheel. 'Thank you.'

It wasn't exactly the immediate easing of tensions that he'd hoped it would be. Hell, if she was strung any tighter she'd explode. 'Only we haven't really talked about how we're going to handle it. You know, now that we're working so closely together, and maybe we should because I feel like we've got off on the wrong foot.'

Considering they hadn't put a foot wrong when they'd just been two strangers on a train, their missteps since had been ridiculous.

'I was planning on ignoring it.'

Callum surprised himself with a laugh at her candour. He didn't think she'd meant it to be funny—more like a morose statement of fact—but it was. 'Yeah. So was I.' But neither of them were doing a very good job. 'And then…'

He stopped himself before the words he'd been about to say slipped out of his mouth. They clearly hadn't been through his rigorous filter. It must be the after-effects of the incense. Or maybe the very present effects of her perfume. It was the one she'd been wearing *that* night. He hadn't really noticed it at the time but right now it was achingly familiar, taking him right back.

She turned her head and their eyes met. 'And then, what?'

His gaze dropped to her mouth. He should leave it alone. Tell her it didn't matter. Walk it back. But the air in the car grew heavier as the space between them seemed to shrink and the urge to pull her ponytail loose slithered thick and dangerous through a head teeming with very bad ideas.

'And then you said Meryl reads auras and had this little half-smile on your mouth like you just knew it was going to throw me, and it was so damn sexy all I could think about was kissing you.'

'Oh. Right,' she muttered, her gaze falling to *his* mouth now. 'That doesn't really help.'

Callum shook his head and somehow, when he stopped, it had inched closer to hers. 'Not even a bit?' Her perfume filled his head and he could see the movement of her throat as she swallowed.

'I think what happened on the train should stay on the train,' she said, her voice husky.

'I agree.' And he did. Or he had, anyway.

'I mean it was…lovely but—'

'Lovely?' His gaze locked with hers as he quirked an eyebrow at the insipid description. 'Why don't you go all the way and tell me it was *nice*?'

She shrugged. 'It was that too.'

But that smile was there on her mouth again and heat flared in his belly. He gave a playful groan. 'You make it sound like we held hands and sang "Kumbayah" all night.'

She laughed, that great big sound she'd used so frequently when they'd been on the train but he hadn't heard since. 'How would you describe it?'

It was a leading question and they were playing with fire. He wondered if she understood how slim the thread was to which he was clinging. But she was looking at his mouth once more and he was pretty sure she'd angled her head closer because he hadn't moved a muscle this time.

In fact, he was barely even breathing.

'Hot,' he muttered, his voice thick in his throat, his gaze dropping to her mouth. 'Sexy. Mind-blowing.'

'Erotic,' she whispered, her pupils dilated.

Callum nodded as he lifted his hand and pushed back an escaped honey-blonde tendril. His fingers whispered across her cheek and jaw as they withdrew. '*So* erotic.'

'Oh, God,' she moaned, her voice low and needy like it'd been when he'd first slipped inside her. Her hands went to the lapels of his jacket and tugged.

Callum didn't need any more encouragement, his mouth meeting hers like they'd never been apart. Like they'd picked up where they'd left off at hot, sexy and mind-blowing, heading straight for erotic.

She smelled good and tasted better and he slid his palms onto her face, holding her steady so he could kiss her harder, deeper, wetter. He ran his tongue over her bottom lip and when she moaned and moved closer still, he thrust it fully into her mouth, his erection surging as her tongue stroked against his.

His heart pounded in his chest, his pulse whooshed like Niagara Falls through his ears and his breathing went from husky to laboured as his whole world narrowed down to just her. Her mouth. Her kisses. Her moans and sighs. The desperate grip of her hands on his lapels.

Just Felicity. In his arms. Again.

And God alone knew where it would have ended up had there not been a firm rap on Felicity's window that scared the life out of him and her also, if the way she grabbed at her chest as they broke apart was any indication.

He was expecting to see half the town with pitchforks out to save St Felicity from his clutches but it was just Mrs Smith from across the road, who'd introduced herself the day he'd moved in and had given him a friendly wave every day since.

She didn't look so friendly now.

'My God,' Felicity muttered under her breath. 'I think I just had a heart attack.'

Callum knew how she felt. What the hell was he doing? He was too old to be necking in cars, for crying out loud. They both were.

Certainly too damn old to be sprung doing it.

'Mrs Smith,' Felicity said, as she wound her window down.

Callum admired the note of cheerful innocence in her voice like nothing was going on here. Like maybe his neighbour hadn't noticed she'd had her tongue down his throat. But the delicious vibrato in her voice betrayed how very much *had* been going on.

'*Flick Mitchell,*' Mrs Smith said, a scandalised note raising her voice to a higher register. 'Dr Hollingsworth.' Her tone for him was rather more accusatory. 'This is hardly appropriate behaviour in broad daylight. I don't need to tell you that Vickers Hill prides itself on public decorum. Just because your parents don't live here any more doesn't mean you should let your behavioural standards slide. It's important to always act like a lady, Flick. I know your mother taught you that.'

It was on the tip of Callum's tongue to tell the old biddy he was more interested in Felicity being a *woman* than a lady but Felicity was nodding her head and saying, 'You're right, Mrs Smith, I'm terribly sorry. You have my assurance it won't happen again.'

Mrs Smith peered down her nose at him. 'And what about your assurances, young man?'

It had been a long time since anyone had called Callum *young man*. He was just getting used to Bill calling him *son*.

Anyone would think they'd been accosted by an angry father with a shotgun instead of a little old lady from across the street, and a dozen different responses flipped through his head. They all died on his lips as Felicity turned pleading eyes on him.

Hell. He was a sucker for that look. Who was he kidding? He was a sucker for any way her face looked. He gritted his teeth and put his hand on his heart. 'I promise there will be no more public displays of affection between Felicity and myself, Mrs Smith.'

Because next time he'd make damn sure he dragged her inside first. Away from prying eyes.

She nodded, satisfied, but wasn't finished with them yet. 'I guess you'll be going home now,' she said pointedly.

'Yes.' Felicity nodded. 'Callum was just leaving.'

Callum didn't want to leave. He very much wanted to finish off the kiss that had been so rudely interrupted. But it was obvious the mood was in tatters and Mrs Smith wasn't going anywhere until *he* did. He glanced at Felicity, who lifted one shoulder in a slight *it's-not-worth-the-aggro* shrug.

'Right,' he said, reaching for the handle. 'I'll…see you tomorrow.'

She nodded but refused to meet his eyes. The last thing he saw as she drove away, apart from Mrs Smith's evil eye, was Felicity's stony profile.

They were back to square one. Worse than square one. If the kiss had been one step forward, this was definitely two steps back.

'Oh, God,' Felicity groaned into her mobile phone a few hours later. 'This is *so* bad. I'm never going to live this down. Why did it have to be Mrs Smith? Now the whole town's going to know. They'll have us married off by the end of next week.'

Luci's laughter floated down the line to her. She'd rung half an hour ago ostensibly to check on the house but also to grill Felicity over a little rumour she'd heard, courtesy of her mother. Poor Luci hadn't been able to get a word in edgewise over Felicity's self-flagellation.

'I say screw the town and just go for it.'

Felicity blinked. 'Well, look at you. Only a short time in the big city and you're completely corrupted. Mrs Smith would be horrified.'

Another laugh. 'Hey, haven't you been telling me to go for it? To move, to have an adventure, to get out of my rut? The same can be said for you, missy. It's been four years since Ned. You deserve a rampant public display of affection and you're twenty-eight years old, for God's sake. Unless…he is a good kisser, right?'

Good? The man was *sublime.* He must have been standing at the top of the queue when they'd been handing out the kissing gene. Ned had been a great kisser too so her bar was set very high. 'Ooh, yeah.'

'Oh, *really*? That good, huh?'

'Well…a girl doesn't like to kiss and tell.'

Which was a good reminder that Callum had said the same thing and there wasn't a lot she could tell Luci without telling her everything and she wasn't ready to do that yet. She didn't want to make it a thing.

The man was here for eight weeks—not someone to blow her precious reputation on. Plus his bedside manner kinda sucked and she was confused as to why something that should have been a major turn-off didn't seem to matter where her body was concerned.

'Anyway, I've been gabbing on and on about me and I haven't even asked you what's going on with you. How's Sydney? Tell me about Seb.'

'Oh, I hardly ever see him,' Luci dismissed airily.

Felicity had known her friend long enough to hear the tell-tale waver in her voice, indicating she wasn't being entirely honest, but Luci ploughed on, talking about her course and Sydney and the weather and her work, and Felicity let her go on while her mind churned through bigger issues.

Like why the hell she'd let Callum kiss her in broad daylight. The fact that she'd actually initiated it by pulling on his lapels was something she chose not to focus on.

She'd been cranky that he'd invaded her space today. After three frustrating clinics on the run, every second of which she'd wanted to shake him for his efficiency over humanity approach, she'd needed some time out.

And then he'd made that comment about Meryl. Although, to be fair, Meryl had been called much worse things than colourful and Felicity's irritation had, in truth, been more about her blemished aura and Meryl's predictions.

Most of the town thought Meryl was certifiable but she'd been right too many times for Felicity to discount.

So why, if she'd been so damn cranky at him, had she kissed him? In broad daylight? Blemishing much more than her aura?

And how was Vickers Hill going to react?

CHAPTER EIGHT

By THE TIME Monday rocked around again Felicity was on her last nerve. Between the speculation that was running rife in Vickers Hill—phone calls from her mother, whispers at the supermarket, unsolicited advice from just about everybody—and enduring another afternoon clinic with Callum's same robotic approach, she was just about done cutting him slack.

If they hadn't kissed on Thursday and tripped the Vickers Hill grapevine into overdrive, she may well have bitten her tongue for longer—it wasn't her place to comment on how he did his job. But they had and Felicity was just about out of her be-nice-to-the-locum store.

It was ironic that everyone thought they were having wild monkey sex when all she wanted to do was strangle him with his stethoscope.

Yeah, the man could kiss. But he *sucked* at connecting with his patients.

It was the last straw when Callum asked her to 'Send in the bunions when you're ready' as she was opening the office door to show a patient out. Felicity's vision went a hot, hazy red as her brain exploded and practically leaked out her ears. She slapped the door shut with the palm of her hand and turned on a dime to glare at him.

'Mr Dunnich,' she said, shoving her hand on her hip.

He glanced up at her from his screen and she hated the way her heart did a funny little leap as he peered at her through those sexy, rimless frames.

'He's the bunions?'

'No,' she said, her voice register sitting squarely in the

frosty zone. 'He's *Mr Dunnich*. That's his name. Or Alf if you're ever invited to be that familiar.' Felicity doubted he would be. 'He's the one whose wife insisted he bring you roses last week, remember?'

'Oh. Yes...'

He was eyeing her warily now. It was obvious he knew he'd done something wrong but equally obvious that he was clueless as to what.

'She had a stroke two years ago and now he's her full-time carer,' Felicity continued, her voice low from the rough edge of emotion that had welled out of nowhere in her chest. 'The roses give her so much pleasure and he knows it.' Her voice cracked and she didn't care how insane she sounded.

Mr Dunnich wasn't just bunions to her.

Callum stood, his forehead crinkling. 'Is there something wrong, Felicity?'

'The person who was just in here with the *hamstring* is called *Malcolm*. The person before that with the *carpal tunnel* is *Stefanie*.'

Pressure built in Felicity's chest as her desperation for him to understand mixed with the emotions she always felt when she was talking about her patients. She sucked in a breath and blew it noisily out of her mouth before she totally broke down and her message was lost amidst incoherent accusations and ugly snot crying.

'They all have names. We don't refer to our patients as their body parts around here. They're *people*, not medical conditions.'

'God...sorry.' He grimaced, pulling his glasses off and throwing them on the table. 'I'm still adjusting to a new mindset. It's a bad habit.'

'Well, break it,' she snapped. Felicity understood that a lot of surgeons had that mindset. But a lot didn't so it was a choice. A bad one.

His jaw clenched. If Felicity hadn't gone to the dark side

she'd have recognised it as a sign to back off. But this had been brewing for a week and she was all-in now.

'Have there been complaints?' he demanded, hands on hips.

'No. Country people don't complain, Callum. They endure. But these are *my* people. They're going to be here long after you swan off back to Sydney and I'm not going to sit around and watch you treat them so impersonally because you're too...'

A thousand adjectives came to mind, pumping through her head as quickly as her blood pumped through her chest. Some glimmer of propriety did prevail, however. 'Too... *cavalier* to take a personal interest in them.'

His green eyes turned to flinty chips of jade. 'I would defy *anybody* to say I haven't given them the very best treatment. I've been thorough and efficient and effective and I *really* don't like your tone.'

'What? Your city surgical nurses don't call you out on your behaviour?' she demanded, keeping her voice low, aware there was a waiting room full of people outside and very thin walls.

'I think they have a little more respect for their colleagues.'

'Oh, really? Well, guess what? You have to earn respect out here. It's not just given to you like some damn golden halo from on high. It takes more than a pair of scrubs and I *will* advocate for my patients whether you like it or not. I've been biting my tongue for a week now but no more.'

'This?' he said, shaking his head in obvious disbelief. '*This* is why you've been angry at me for a week?'

'What? A little too trivial for you?'

He shook his head at her, his mouth a flat line. 'Oh, well, please,' he said, his tone bitingly sarcastic, 'by all means do let me have it all. I'd hate you to pop a lung keeping it all in.'

Felicity wasn't sure about popping a lung but she sure as hell felt like she was about to blow a vessel in her brain as her blood pressure hit stroke levels. She stalked over to his desk and stabbed her finger at the woodgrain surface.

'It's not about efficiency. There's more to being a good family practice doctor than thoroughness. A GP role is about *connection* and forming long-term *relationships.* It's about *community* and earning trust so that people can and *will* tell you stuff that they'd never tell anyone else because you're their doctor and they're scared out of their brains about something. For Pete's sake.' She shook her head. 'Don't they teach you any of this in GP school? Or does the big hot-shot city surgeon not need to listen?'

'Of course,' he snapped. 'I'm just not...the touchy-feely type.'

'You don't *have* to be. But you can't be robotic about it either. You're just going through the motions at the moment, Callum. Ticking the boxes. Frankly, your bedside manner sucks.'

'Oh, no.' He shook his head vehemently. 'It damn well does not. My bedside manner is great. *All* my patients love me.'

'Well, I'm sure they do when you're talking to them post-op when they're high on drugs and whatever surgical miracle you've performed for them.'

'Oh, yeah?' he snorted. 'This from St Felicity.'

Felicity had no clue what he meant but she wasn't about to get distracted from her point.

'Seriously. Just think about it for a moment. How much *actual* time would you spend with each patient, not counting the hours you're cutting them open? An hour? Two? In general practice, if you stick around a place long enough you're going to see that person multiple times over many years for a variety of different things. You're going to be there with them through good and bad, thick and thin. You're going to tell them they're pregnant or miscarrying, or have cancer or are in remission. You're the person they're going to trust with their lives. The one they're going to break down in front of and who they're going to look at with eyes that are desperate for answers and cures you just don't have.'

Felicity's breath caught as her throat thickened. Damn it. She was getting emotional again. But this stuff meant something.

'They *have* to be more than the sum of their parts to you, Callum. *That's* what being a good GP is about. Forget what they taught you in surgical school. None of it is relevant here.'

Even as she said the words she realised that was the crux of the problem for him. This career move had been forced on him by his eye injury and clearly his heart wasn't in it. It was a fall-back position for him, not a calling. Not like it was for Bill and Angela and Meera.

All the rage and anger that had buoyed her to say what she'd been itching to say flowed out of her, leaving her curiously deflated. 'Why are you even here, Callum? Is it really what you want? You don't seem to be very invested in the job and you're a long way from home so I'm wondering if maybe you're just running away?'

'No.' He shook his head. 'I'm not running away. I just needed a…circuit-breaker. A fresh start. Some clear air for a while. But I am going back. I *will* go back.'

Felicity studied his face. It was so grim and determined it spoke volumes. 'To prove yourself?'

He didn't admit it but she could tell by the tightening of his face that she'd hit close to the bone. 'You have a problem with that?' he asked, his tone defensive.

'No.' And she didn't. But it was fair warning. The man was good-looking. A great kisser. And knew how to melt her into a puddle in bed. It would be easy to get swept away by that and forget he didn't want this job or small-town life.

'But why become a GP? You could have retrained in another surgical speciality. Something that doesn't require a lot of precision. Orthopaedics. All hammer and chisels and power tools. Lot of grunt. Very manly.'

He laughed and it helped to ease the tension. Felicity was relieved. She'd been pretty harsh on him.

'Even that involves a degree of microsurgery and I just can't trust myself.'

'So become a physician. Plenty of specialties to sink your teeth into.'

He shook his head again. His frame was erect, his head was held high, but there was defeat in his gaze. 'I can't work in a hospital. There's that smell, you know?' He looked at her earnestly and Felicity nodded. She knew that smell. Like it had been scrubbed with disinfectant only seconds before you walked into it.

'I love that smell. It's been running through my veins since I was a kid. It's addictive. And it's associated with surgery to me. Having to set foot in a hospital every day for work and not go to the operating theatres would be torture. A constant reminder of everything I've lost. That I'm living out the consolation prize instead of the dream. I can't do it.'

Part of Felicity wanted to tell him to harden up. That life wasn't fair. That it threw you curveballs. But she figured he'd learned that lesson plenty over the last couple of years.

'So you chose general practice.'

'Yes.'

And here they were.

'So *choose* it,' she said.

'Okay, fine,' he huffed, sitting in his chair, rubbing a hand over his eyes. 'What do you suggest to improve my skills? Teach me.'

She narrowed her eyes at him. 'Seriously? It's not rocket science.'

'Seriously. I mean it.' He nodded. 'Give me some pointers and I'll employ them for the remaining patients today. You can critique me at the end. Give me a score out of ten.'

Felicity suppressed an eye-roll. Just like a man to make it competitive. But she had to give him chops for taking what she'd said on board. Especially given its level of frankness.

She'd known some surgeons in Adelaide who would have had apoplexy if she'd spoken to them the way she'd spoken to Callum.

The fact he seemed keen to improve was also encouraging.

'Fine.' A stray piece of her fringe fell over her right eye and she absently blew it away as she pulled up a chair.

'How about you start by calling them by their names? And *thinking* about them that way too. As *people* first. And instead of focusing on their problem and trying to solve it as soon as possible, then calling out "Next", like you've set a mental timer, maybe you could try a little conversation. Talk to *them* when they're here, *not* your computer screen, and about something other than whatever it is they're coming in for. The weather. The weekend markets. Their kids. Their grandkids. Their mothers-in-law. Harvest season. Mulberry pies. Anything.'

'Conversation, huh?'

Felicity heard the amusement in his voice and couldn't stop the smile that curved her mouth. She had first-hand experience of how good he was at conversation. 'Yeah. It's okay, we have time. Pretend you're on a train.'

He smiled too and she breathed in sharply as his whole damn face came alive. For a moment they just sat there smiling at each other, Felicity's hopes and *heart* floating foolishly outside her body somewhere. 'Who knows, you might even discover you *like* being a GP.'

His smile faded a little, a good reminder that Callum was only temporary and not to get carried away. Not to let herself become some kind of consolation prize—his words.

'How about we start with Mr Dunnich?' she said, forcing her legs to stand and dropping her gaze to her trousers, where she brushed at invisible creases.

'The bunions?'

Her head snapped up to find him grinning big and wide. The kind of grin that made Felicity wish she was still seated.

'And the roses,' he added quickly. 'And the wife with a stroke who he cares for. And adores.'

Felicity refused to laugh but she had to fight the urge as she nodded in acknowledgement. 'Correct.'

Callum felt suitably chastised as he waited for Felicity to get Mr Dunnich. If he'd known this was what had been bugging her all week he'd have had it out with her sooner. On Friday and again today he'd figured it was the kiss.

It was almost a relief it had been about this.

The fact the entire town thought he'd besmirched St Flick was way beyond his scope of practise but the way he interacted with patients he could fix. The practical experience he'd had during his training had been very different from Vickers Hill. Most of his practical had been at the busy north shore practice he was heading to in the New Year. Scheduling was always tight and that's how he'd learned.

Get them in, get them out. *Next.*

He'd even been applauded for it.

The fact that it wasn't the way they did things here hadn't even occurred to him and he was grateful to Felicity for finally mentioning it.

Or perhaps cracking up about it was a better descriptor.

She'd asked him if a city nurse had ever called him on his behaviour and the truth was a nurse probably wouldn't have dared talk to him like that in one of his theatres. He'd been the surgeon and he'd ruled the kingdom. Not only that, he came from a long line of surgeons. The Hollingsworth name was well known in Sydney. And he'd been the heir apparent for a long time.

God. He sounded like an arrogant douche.

The door opened, pulling Callum out of his reverie. 'Ah, Mr Dunnich.' Callum half rose. 'Come and sit down.'

Mr Dunnich approached more tentatively than he had last time and Callum cringed internally. He'd been too busy at the computer to acknowledge Mr Dunnich last time until he had sat down and it was clear the man was wary of him.

Callum smiled and indicated a chair for his patient. 'How are you?' he asked as the old man sat.

Mr Dunnich shot a glance at Felicity, as if he was waiting for an interpretation. 'Fine, thank you, Doctor.'

Callum grimaced at how formal Mr Dunnich was this time. No *Doc* today. The fact that he was responsible for it didn't sit well at all. He obviously had some ground to make up and he was determined to do just that.

'How are the toes going?'

Mr Dunnich bent to take off his shoes. 'Much better,' he said. 'Those pills worked a treat.'

Callum performed the same examination on the toes as he'd done last week but this time, aware of Felicity's scrutiny, he commented on his patient's neatly pressed trousers. 'That's a perfect crease you've got going on there.'

'Oh...yes.'

'Do you get them dry-cleaned or iron them yourself?'

'Do it myself,' he said, pride strengthening his voice. 'Twenty years in the army when I was a lad. Some things you never forget.'

'Really? I might have to drop mine around too.'

Mr Dunnich glanced at him awkwardly and Callum grinned and winked. He was relieved when the old man and then Felicity laughed. 'Me too,' she added.

'Not on your life.' Mr Dunnich chortled.

'Please thank your wife for the roses last week. I took them home and they were perfect in Luci's house.'

'Oh, yes,' Mr Dunnich agreed cheekily. 'Luci's house was made for roses.'

'Does your wife have a favourite?' Callum enquired as he indicated Mr Dunnich should put his shoes back on.

'No. No one in particular but she does love the climbing roses best. Every morning without fail we have a cuppa out on the front porch so she can look out over the arbour where they all climb. Gets some Vitamin D too before the day becomes too hot. Except the last few days. Lizzy hasn't really wanted to.'

Callum frowned. 'Is she sick?'

'No, I don't think so,' he said, straightening now his shoes were back on. 'Communication has been hard since the stroke but I've got pretty good at understanding her. She says not. I think she's just kinda down, you know? I'm a little bit worried about her, to be honest. She's never been that kind of person.'

'That's no good.' Callum's medical antennae pinged. It had been such a long time since they'd done that. It was nice to have them back.

He flicked a glance at Felicity. Her brows were drawn together in a concerned V. Maybe Mrs Dunnich needed to be checked on. 'How about we add Lizzy to Felicity's home visit list on Thursday? Just to give her a once-over, put your mind at ease?'

Mr Dunnich brightened. 'Yeah?'

'Absolutely, Mr Dunnich,' Felicity confirmed. 'We're here to support you and Lizzy.'

'Okay, then, thank you. I'd really appreciate it. I'll make you some of Lizzy's rhubarb tartlets. I've got rhubarb coming out of my ears.'

'That sounds fabulous,' she agreed, and Callum wondered where the hell she put all that food if every Thursday was the same as the last one. Her figure was about as perfect as it got without a single sign of twelve different carbohydrate-laden snacks.

'Right, then, it's settled,' Callum said. 'Now, I think I'll write you up for a month's worth of the medication for your bunions and let's assess again after that. Sooner, of course, if the pain worsens. Does that sound like a plan?'

'Sure does, Doc.'

Callum couldn't deny how satisfying that *Doc* was as

he turned to the computer and ordered the medication, the script printing out quickly. He pulled it out of the printer and handed it to Mr Dunnich, standing at the same time.

'See you next month, Mr Dunnich,' Callum said. 'And Felicity will see you on Thursday.'

'Call me Alf,' he said, also rising and holding out his hand, which Callum took. 'I'll make sure to have some extra tartlets for Flick to give to you.'

Callum smiled. The people of Vickers Hill obviously prided themselves on the gourmet reputation of the town, nestled as it was in the middle of wine country. They also seemed intent on making him fat.

'Or she might just keep them for herself,' Felicity said. Mr Dunnich laughed as amusement lit Felicity's eyes and they dared him to surrender to his fate.

'Rhubarb tartlets are my favourite. I would love that.'

Callum let out a breath as he sat at his desk after Alf left with Felicity. If the shine in her eyes was anything to go by, he'd nailed it. There had certainly been no tight-lipped, jaw-clenched, silent disapproval.

The door opened and he braced himself for his next patient—a torn ACL. *Oops.* No. *Jane Richie* was his next patient. But he needn't have worried, it was just Felicity.

'Now,' she said as she walked towards him with an I-told-you-so swagger. 'That wasn't so hard, was it?'

He rolled his eyes. 'You're a gloater, aren't you?'

'I have no idea what you mean,' she said, batting her eyelashes at him in an exaggerated manner with a big grin that transformed her entire face, and in that moment he saw the same thing that everyone else around here did—Flick, who was all things to all people. Who was popular with everybody and loved by all.

Who belonged to them.

It was a sobering thought. She'd been the girl on the train

to him since the beginning but seeing her here in her natural habitat it was clear that train girl had been the aberration.

Still, he wasn't ready to let that version of her go either. There were obviously two sides to Felicity and he was privileged to have seen the side that obviously no one here had. 'Let me make it up to you for being so obtuse and… What was it you called me? Cavalier? Come to my place for dinner tonight. I'm a pretty mean cook.'

The remnants of her smile slid from her mouth as she sat on the chair Mr Dunnich had just vacated. 'No.'

'*Just* dinner.'

'No.'

'Are you worried about Mrs Smith?'

'No. I'm worried about us. Together. Alone. Somewhere near a bed.'

A thick slug of desire hit Callum low in the belly. He'd been thinking about them alone *on* a bed an inordinate amount of time ever since the kiss in the car. 'You think I can't control myself?'

'I think you know as well as I do that *neither* of us will be able to control ourselves.'

Callum liked it that she wasn't playing coy or trying to pretend there wasn't a thing simmering between them. She may have been trying to ignore it for a week but she wasn't in denial.

'And we're not going there.'

He frowned, getting his thoughts back on track. 'We're not?' It was the right thing to do given they had to work together and he was here for only a short period of time but…

'No. I'm going to be your friend.'

Callum didn't have many female friends. The ones he did have he didn't want to sleep with.

The same couldn't be said for Felicity.

'You are?'

'Yes. I'll take you touring on the weekends. We'll visit some art galleries and antique shops. There's some great lookouts and a heritage trail. We'll drink wine and eat gourmet food at a bunch of different wineries. It'll be fun.'

Not as much fun as drinking wine and eating gourmet food off her body. 'Okay...'

'Are you free on Saturday?'

'Yes.'

'Good. I'll pick you up at eleven.'

CHAPTER NINE

FELICITY WASN'T NERVOUS when she picked Callum up on Saturday. She was confident they could be friends, despite the very definite tug of her libido and crazy speculation from the entire town.

Her libido didn't rule her actions and the town could talk all they wanted. Felicity knew from old they would anyway. As long as she and Callum knew where they stood, the town could go on building castles in the air.

Of course, the second she saw him walking down Luci's flower-lined pathway her confidence nosedived. She didn't know if it was the riot of colour and prettiness all around him making him seem so damn male or the way he filled out his snug blue jeans, but her belly looped the loop.

Friends. She could do this. *They* could do it.

They had to. Vickers Hill was not the place to be reckless. To be the girl from the train. She would be here long after he'd left and she didn't want to be walking around with everyone talking about her behind her back. She didn't want to be an object of gossip or, worse, pity.

Besides, sex was easy. A friendship could be more enduring and, she suspected, less pain in the long run. Above all else, she sensed that Callum needed a friend more than anything now. He'd been through a lot and was still working things out. She had no doubt he could find lovers. But he was in Vickers Hill for a reason—for clear air.

Sex would just fog it all up.

Felicity braced herself as he opened the car door and climbed in beside her. She smiled and said, 'Hi,' trying not to notice the way his T-shirt fell against his stomach. It was difficult when she knew exactly what was beneath.

'Hey,' he said. She couldn't really see his eyes behind the dark sunglasses but she could feel them all over her. 'You look great.'

Felicity blushed, reminding her of how he'd made her blush on the train. She was wearing a dress she'd bought at Bondi with Luci. It was strappy and light in an Aztec pattern, baring her shoulders and arms. The skirt was loose and flowing, the hem fluttering around her knees.

'Thanks,' she murmured, returning her attention to the road as she engaged the clutch. She wasn't going to tell him he looked great too. She hadn't bought him here to flirt with him and if she said, 'You don't look so bad either', that's what she'd be doing.

She didn't want the time he had left here to be one long slow tease between the two of them until one, or both, of them cracked. She was genuine about forming a friendship with him. Absolutely certain that it was their destiny.

Or, if nothing else, sensible.

'Where are we off to?'

'Pretty Maids All In A Row cellar door,' Felicity said, pleased to be slipping into tour-guide mode. It was a role she often played for visitors. She loved Vickers Hill and the entire Clare Valley. It may be smaller and further away than the renowned wine-growing region of the Barossa but it was known for its foodie culture and many high-end restaurants.

'That sounds like a mouthful.'

'It is a little.' She laughed. 'But they have a Riesling to die for and my favourite menu of all the local wineries. They do this rabbit dish that will make you weep. But first I'm going to take you on a bit of a scenic drive around.'

'Sounds good to me.' He nodded. 'Lead on.'

By the time Felicity pulled into the winery car park an hour later she didn't think she'd laughed so much in her life. Cal-

lum had been an entertaining companion—very *Cal*like—
as she'd driven him all around the valley to give him a good
overview of the district that surrounded Vickers Hill.

During lunch—rabbit and a very fine Riesling—they
talked a lot of shop. Callum was keen to know all the ins
and outs of the practice and the different relationships and
Felicity was happy to impart all she knew.

It was only when they were relaxing over dessert and
she was feeling the buzz from her second glass of wine that
things turned personal.

'So how come,' he asked, supporting his chin in his palm
as he leaned his elbow on the thick slab of timber that made
up the table, 'somebody hasn't snapped you up by now, St
Felicity.'

Felicity laughed. 'St Felicity?'

'Yes. *Saint.*' He grinned. 'Vickers Hill's very own. You're
the woman who can do no wrong, don't you know? I have
a feeling that the town will apply to have you canonised
any day now.'

If he only knew how very unsaintly her thoughts had
been today he'd be shocked. 'I think I have to be dead for
that to happen.'

'A trifling detail,' he dismissed with a flick of his hand.
'Seriously, though, were you born in Vickers Hill? Because
your people do love you.'

'Born, bred and schooled. Stayed here until I left to go
to uni in Adelaide to study nursing.'

'And you came straight back and have dedicated every
waking moment of your life to the good people of the Hill?'

Felicity laughed. 'No. I've only been back for four years.
I worked in Adelaide for just over seven years.'

'Whereabouts?'

'At the general hospital, in their emergency department.'

'And you came home because you were...' He raised both
eyebrows. 'Over it?' She shook her head. 'Burned out?' She

shook it again. 'I know,' he said, smiling, drawing attention to his lips, 'St Felicity was sacked.'

'No.' She laughed.

'It was drugs, wasn't it? It's okay, you can tell. You're secret is safe with me.'

'No,' she said, laughing harder. 'Try again.'

'Hmm.' He narrowed his eyes, his gaze roaming all over her face for long moments. 'I know,' he announced. 'It was because of a man, wasn't it? He broke your heart.'

Felicity's breath hitched at his startling accuracy. She hoped her face didn't betray how badly her heart had been broken as she forced joviality into her voice. 'Bingo.'

Callum's face morphed from teasing to serious in one second flat. 'Oh, God, sorry. I didn't mean... I shouldn't have been kidding around. That was...dumb.'

'It's fine. It was four years ago. I'm over it.'

It was a startling revelation to realise she *was* over it. The hurt had lingered for such a long time. But she could put her hand on her heart right here, right now and honestly say that all the feelings she'd had for Ned were no more.

She'd always *love* him in that nostalgic we-were-good-to-gether-and-you-used-to-mean-the-world-to-me way. They'd had a lot of great times. There'd been a lot of love. But she was over the heart*ache*.

She was healed. And not crazy glued back together but actually fully knitted.

'How long were you together?'

'Four years. He—Ned—was a nurse. We went through uni together and we both worked in A and E. We were friends first and it kind of developed slowly from there. Crept up on us, I guess.'

'So how did it all go wrong? What happened?'

To this day, Felicity still didn't fully understand it. It had been so sudden. 'One day he just said he'd met somebody else. Just...' Felicity splayed her hands '...like that. We were a few weeks off taking a holiday to New Zealand. I thought he was going to propose.' She gave a half-laugh and shook her head, thinking about how damn clueless she'd been. 'On the day he dumped me I was asking him if his passport had arrived yet and he just blurted it out. "I've met somebody else and I want to be with her."'

His hand slid across the table and covered hers. 'I'm so sorry. That must have been devastating. What a total creep.'

His quick insult surprised a laugh out of Felicity. 'He said he hadn't meant it to happen, he hadn't been looking for it. For what it's worth, I believed him. He was never the kind of guy who was always looking over my shoulder, you know?'

He winced. 'We're all creeps, aren't we?' He withdrew his hand and placed both of them over his heart. 'I sincerely apologise on behalf of the entire male sex in that case.'

She laughed again. 'It's okay. I survived.'

'You did,' he murmured, his gaze locking on hers as he dropped his hands to the table. 'Kudos to you.'

'Oh, I licked my wounds for a long time, don't you worry about that. It was pretty messy for a while.'

'Did you never suspect?'

'Never.' Felicity had been completely blindsided by Ned's admission. 'Apparently he'd known her for a month.'

He blinked. 'Wow. That's a *big* call.'

'Yeah. But they got married a month later and have two kids so they must be doing something right.'

'And you came home?'

Felicity nodded. 'I did. Home to my old bedroom and my father's country music playing on the radio and my mother's home cooking.'

'Just what the doctor ordered,' he teased.

'Yes.' She'd put on six kilos in that first month. It had taken her another year to get them off. 'Then Dr Dawson gave me a job, even though I had no practice nurse qualifications. Sure, I'm Luci's friend so he knew me well and probably couldn't say no to me when I burst into tears in front of him one day, but I will be forever in his debt for that. He was a saviour. *Work* was a saviour.'

Work had got her through days when all she'd wanted to do was curl up in a ball. It had saved her from ringing Ned a hundred times a day, screaming and/or crying at him until she was hoarse.

'You were lucky, then.'

His voice was even but there was a gravity to his words and all the teasing light had dimmed from his eyes. Of course. Callum had never had that when his life had gone pear-shaped. She'd relied on work to get her through her grief but he hadn't been *able* to work. The mere fact he *couldn't* had been at the very crux of his grief.

'Yeah, I was,' she agreed.

'Well,' he said, tossing his head as if he was trying to shake off the black cloud that had descended around them, 'for what it's worth, I'm glad you weren't with that lying, cheating scumbag the day you stepped on the train.'

Felicity laughed. 'So am I.' The heaviness of the conversation suddenly lightened as good memories crowded out the bad. Sitting opposite him now, it felt like they were back in the dining carriage.

'What about you?' she asked. 'A woman ever broken your heart? No.' She shook her head. 'Let me guess. You do all the breaking, I bet.'

'I'll have you know a girl called Susie Watts smashed my heart to smithereens when I was nine years old.' He put a hand on his chest. 'She dumped me for Jimmy Jones because he had a bigger bicycle than I did.'

Felicity sucked in some air through her hollowed cheeks in an appropriately sympathetic noise. 'Ouch.' But the urge to laugh was overwhelming. 'I'm sorry. That's awful.'

He narrowed his eyes. 'You don't look very sorry.'

Laughter bubbled in her chest. 'No, I was just thinking...'

'Thinking what?'

'A guy called Jimmy Jones? He sounds like one of those

bad boys some girls are fatally attracted to. Maybe it wasn't just his bicycle that was bigger.'

'Oh, no,' Callum groaned good-naturedly, shutting his eyes before opening them again. 'Kick a guy when he's down.'

She did laugh this time. 'Sorry,' she said, trying to make herself stop.

He drank his coffee and watched her patiently—intently—a smile turning the fullness of his lips into two plush crescents. God, he was *sexy*. The way he smiled was sexy. The way his hair brushed his ears was sexy. The way he tilted his head was sexy.

The way he looked at *her* was sexy.

'So, you didn't answer my question,' Felicity said when she'd pulled herself under control. 'Ever had your heart broken? In an *adult* relationship?'

He placed his coffee cup back on its saucer. 'Not really.'

'You more a play-the-field kind of guy?' Everything about him oozed masculine confidence. She could see him at some hip Sydney bar mobbed by women.

'There's been a couple of longer-term relationships but they were never love matches and when you're working long hours and studying all the other hours left in the day they tend to take a back seat until they fizzle out. They were light and fun and mutually enjoyable while they lasted. And then...'

Felicity waited for him to continue after his abrupt cessation. When he didn't she cocked an eyebrow and prompted him. 'And then?'

He shifted in his seat, sitting more upright, pulling his arm back and propping his bent elbow on the curved back of the chair. 'After the accident...people didn't really know what to say and frankly I was pretty awful to be around sometimes. Most people in my social circle were in medicine and a lot of them dropped out of the circle—I guess because I was the elephant in the room. I was their *what if.*

A rather sad reminder of how you could be riding on top one second then on your butt the next.'

'Did they think it was contagious?' she asked drily.

He smiled. 'I think maybe they thought of me more like a bad omen. Surgeons are all about the successes. We don't like to talk about failures. We certainly don't like to be confronted by them.'

'And it was the same with women?'

'No. Ironically, my sex life had never been better.' He fiddled with his coffee cup for a moment. 'And I'm not very proud to say I kind of drowned myself in that for quite a while.' He shrugged. 'I was throwing myself a huge pity party and it wasn't like there was much else to do. Until I realised that about ninety percent of the action I was getting amounted to *pity* sex.'

'Oh.' Felicity wanted to reach out and touch him like he'd touched her, but he seemed so far away now. 'What about the other ten percent?'

'Some kind of sick sexual healing for the blind man thing.'

Felicity grimaced. 'Oh, dear.'

'Yes.' He frowned into his coffee. 'After that I kind of just stopped. It was a real downer for my libido.'

Felicity knew she shouldn't get into a conversation about his libido in case it veered into flirting territory but she was a sucker for a wounded guy and the nurse inside her urged her to try and turn that frown upside down. Soothe it right off his face.

'Your sex drive seemed in perfect working order to me,' she murmured, hoping her voice sounded light and teasing rather than coy and flirty.

'Ah, well,' he said, lifting his gaze squarely to her lips, sucking away all the oxygen between them, 'that's because you woke it up.'

Her mouth tingled under his intense scrutiny and she could barely breathe. She probably shouldn't feel so damn

turned on, especially as he didn't look entirely happy about
his newly roused libido.

But she did. 'I'm…sorry?'

He shook his head, his eyes lifting higher and locking
with hers. 'I'm not.'

The words both pleased and petrified Felicity. Was it just
a statement of fact or a subtle reminder of the thing they
were trying to ignore? Luckily for her, a waiter chose that
moment to clear their table, breaking their eye contact and
the accompanying tension.

For now.

Felicity pulled her car up outside Luci's house at around
four. She waved at Mrs Smith, who was in her front garden, watering her plants. The old biddy didn't even pretend
to be minding her own business.

'Uh-oh,' Callum said. 'Bouncer at six o'clock.'

Felicity laughed at the idea of Mrs Smith in a black
T-shirt with Security stamped across the front in big white
letters. Not that she needed it—she'd taught at the primary
school for almost thirty years. Nobody in Vickers Hill
messed with her.

'Thank you for today,' Callum said as he undid his seat
belt. 'I had a really great time.'

'So did I.'

And she had. They'd had their moments when teasing
and banter had definitely branched into flirting but they'd
pulled back and just enjoyed each other's company.

As much as two people who were trying to deny their
sexual attraction could.

'We should do it again,' he said.

Felicity nodded. 'Oh, we will. By the time you get out of
here I promise you'll have seen every inch worth seeing.'

She realised the potential double entendre about the same
time as Callum, his eyebrows rising as he tried to suppress
a grin. 'None of those inches include me.'

He laughed. 'Just checking.'

She rolled her eyes at him. 'Seriously? Mrs Smith is over there, probably trying to read our lips, so show a little decorum, please.'

'Of course.' He nodded and moulded his face into solemn lines but there was mischief in his eyes. 'So…my turn for the chauffeuring next time but I can't do next weekend because I'm on call.'

'That's okay. I'm actually going to an art exhibition on Thursday night at Drayton's Crossing. We drove through there on our way to lunch? It's a friend of mine but if you want to come along it should be fun. You can drive if you want.'

'Ah…okay.'

Felicity gave a half-laugh. 'Your enthusiasm is overwhelming. It won't be MOMA but she's really good, I promise. She has sell-out showings in Adelaide but this is a fundraiser for the local fire service and she's a Clare Valley girl.'

'No, it's not that.' He smoothed his palms up and down his jeans, which was distracting as hell. 'I can't…drive at night on my conditional licence. My visual acuity and depth of field in my left eye deteriorates badly in the dark.'

'Oh, okay, sure.' She shrugged. 'So I'll drive. I don't mind.'

But she could tell that *he* minded. *A lot*.

'It's not okay,' he growled, shoving a hand through his hair. 'I feel like a damn teenager on a curfew.'

His frustration was almost palpable. He'd obviously lost a degree of independence as well as his career and Felicity wanted nothing more than to soothe him, but it was probably the last thing *he* wanted from her. A guy like Callum who had turned his back on a steady supply of pity sex probably just needed a bit of understanding.

Being able to jump in a car and drive whenever she

wanted was something she always took for granted. Any restriction on that would be a constant irritant for her too.

'I can imagine that's a real pain in the butt.'

'Yeah,' he huffed, looking out his window for long moments. 'I've got used to taking a taxi everywhere in Sydney.' He glanced at her. 'I don't suppose they have any Ubers in Vickers Hill?'

'Ah, no.' Felicity smiled. 'But we do have an old-fashioned taxi service and I'm perfectly fine to drive us to Drayton's on Thursday, I promise. Hell, this car's been there so many times it could do it without any assistance from me.'

'Fine. But I drive on our next daytime outing.'

Felicity nodded. 'It's a date.' *Damn it.* She cringed at her flippant choice of words, her cheeks heating. Way to make it awkward, Flick. 'Well, you know, *figuratively*, of course.'

He laughed. 'Of course.'

Between that gaffe and Mrs Smith starting to pace up and down her footpath Felicity just wanted today to be over. She'd had a great time but clearly it was only going to be downhill from here.

'Well…I'm pretty sure Mrs Smith is about to turn her hose on us so I think it's time I left.'

'Sure.' He reached for the doorhandle. 'Thanks again.'

He was out of the car before she remembered she hadn't given him the gift from Mr Dunnich. 'Wait,' she called out quickly before he shut the door.

He ducked his head back in the car. 'What? Mrs Smith is giving me the evil eye.'

Felicity smiled. Mrs Smith hadn't lost that school-teacher glare—the one that could see straight through a kid and know exactly what they were guilty of. She reached over to the back seat and grabbed the plastic container with five of the most perfectly formed rhubarb tartlets she'd ever seen.

'This is from Alf. He made me promise I'd give them to you. Not keep them for myself.' She thrust the box of temptation into his hands. 'You have no idea how hard that was.'

'I appreciate your restraint,' he murmured as he took the container, looking at her with eyes that left her in no doubt he appreciated much, much more.

Unexpected heat arced between them like a solar flare. 'Don't,' she said, trying to mentally pull herself back from this different sort of temptation. 'There were six. I ate one.'

He chuckled and it oozed into the car all around her. 'I appreciate your lack of restraint too.'

Felicity's breath caught in her throat as his gaze turned copulatory. Was he thinking about her lack of restraint in bed that night? Because she sure as hell was. She swore she could almost feel the rock of the train around them again.

Then he was straightening, the car *actually* rocking slightly as the door shut. He waved at Mrs Smith, earning himself a scowl, before he swaggered down Luci's path like he was striding along a hospital corridor instead of a path lined with lavender and sweet peas.

Two weeks down. Six more to go.

CHAPTER TEN

THE DAYS FORMED a steady rhythm, which Callum was starting to appreciate. He'd thought he'd needed the pace and the unpredictability of the north shore practice to keep his mind off things. He'd thought if he slowed down, if he had too much time to be idle, he'd have too much time to dwell on the state of his life.

And probably in the city that would have been true.

But there was something surprisingly satisfying about the slower tempo in the country. It took his mind off himself more effectively than keeping a frantic pace ever had because it freed up his mind from multiple foci—a jam-packed appointment book or surgical list to get through each day—and allowed him the space to think more holistically. He wasn't skimming the surface. He had time to sink down deeper into the layers.

He realised now that he hadn't needed to keep physically busy—he'd just needed to be mentally challenged. That was what he'd always loved about surgery—the mental challenge of the detail involved—and now he was finding a similar appreciation in the way general practice involved the minutiae of people's lives. That they were, as Felicity had said, the sum of *all* their parts, not just the product of one.

Even in the mornings, when he wasn't at work, he didn't feel the constant churn of loss and regret that continually threatened to swamp him back home in those rare quiet moments. Life in Sydney and the constant mix of pity and expectation from people for him to *bounce back*, to be the guy he'd been before the accident, seemed a million miles away.

Everything back home had reminded him of what he couldn't have. Everything in Vickers Hill showed him what he *could*.

He'd come here hoping to break the cycle of mental self-flagellation, hoping to shrug off the old skin and grow a new one. A better one. A *thicker* one.

Deep down he hadn't thought that possible.

But as Thursday rocked around and he was lazily appreciating Luci's garden as he sipped his coffee, he was beginning to think it was very much possible. He was even beginning to think it was possible that he and Felicity could be friends.

At work it seemed possible anyway. They were getting on well and it was easy to keep her straight in his head in a place where she was so clearly 'the nurse'. From what she wore to how people treated her to what they called her, everything existed to create that mental barrier.

Everyone called her Flick and every day she was dressed in the same navy pants and polo shirt as the other staff, her hair pulled into the same low ponytail. People spoke to her with both respect and affection. At work she *was* Flick and through tacit agreement they didn't talk about the train or that weird moment in the car on Saturday. They kept things professional, and it worked.

Even the art show tonight was kept in perspective when both Bill and Julia as well as Angela and about a dozen of his patients were also attending. Yes, *she'd* invited him and he was going *with* her but it was merely an act of kindness extended to the newbie in town.

It was the embodiment of country hospitality. An invitation that could have been issued by any one of the practice employees. But it had been issued by her. By *Flick*. And he was looking forward to it immensely.

Unfortunately it wasn't *Flick* who picked him up. It was most definitely *Felicity*. In that little black dress from the train. Or maybe it wasn't the exact one. But it was similar. Figure-hugging, a great glimpse of cleavage, a very distracting bow on the side that looked like it might be the way in—and *out*.

Okay. Not the one from the train—he'd have remembered that bow.

Did she know how tempting that damn bow was? Had she done it on purpose? He supposed there weren't a lot of places or events in Vickers Hill that required dressing up so why wouldn't she when she had the chance? It was obvious from the train that she was as partial to getting all girly as the next woman.

He just wished she'd chosen the light and summery look from the weekend when she'd taken him to lunch at the winery. The whole girl-next-door thing suited her.

There was nothing girl-next-door about this dress.

Not the figure-hugging, not the cleavage, not the sexy high heels. Not that damn bow or the sway of her hips or the swing of her long, loose hair. This was a Pavlov's dog dress.

And he was salivating like crazy.

It certainly drove out the mushrooming frustration he'd felt as he'd waited to be picked up like some teenager who'd had his keys taken off him by his parents. The black cloud that had been building all afternoon had blown right away as he'd opened the door, and by the time he'd slid into the car seat beside her, it was long gone.

Music, low and sweet, flared to life on the radio as she started the engine. Her bangles jingled. Her perfume enveloped him, filling his head with her scent and a string of bad ideas.

'You look…lovely,' he said as she smiled at him.

'Thanks.'

She reached for her seat belt but not before he saw a tiny slip in that smile, a slight dimming of the sparkle in her eyes as she buckled up.

Had she been hoping for more?

Unfortunately, lovely was about as polite as he could get right now. The next level up was *sexy*. The one after that was not for polite company.

He was okay with being friends. He understood the reasons for it and thought it was doable. But he wasn't stupid enough to deny there was the possibility of a very different relationship if they chose to go down that path.

Which they hadn't.

'I'm worried about Lizzy Dunnich,' she said, as she drove off.

Callum dragged his mind out of his—and her—pants. It was hard to concentrate on shop talk when she looked like the woman from the train, but at least it would help him to keep the division between the two very different women straight in his head.

'Is she unwell?' Felicity had obviously decided to keep her on her home-visit schedule after she'd seen her last week.

'No. Nothing specific I can pinpoint. Just a feeling. Like Alf says, she's just really withdrawn. But Bailey—that's their Labrador—has taken to not leaving her side. I'm worried he knows something we don't.'

Callum hadn't owned a dog, growing up, and they'd never come into his realm of practice when he'd been putting on a pair of scrubs every morning, but he'd read enough anecdotal evidence about the canine-human connection to understand why Felicity was worried.

'You think she might be…'

'Yeah.'

The white of her knuckles around the steering wheel drew his attention. *My* people, she'd called them that day she'd finally exploded at him for his poor connection with the patients.

And Mrs Dunnich was one of them.

'She's eighty-six,' he said gently, staring at her profile. 'And she's already had one stroke.'

'Yeah,' she said again, her eyes glued to the road.

He wasn't telling her anything she didn't already know. Lizzy Dunnich didn't have a whole lot of ticks in her column.

But this one felt close to him too.

As a surgeon he'd had patients die. The last one, not long before his accident, had been a fifty-eight-year-old woman who'd presented with a dissecting abdominal aortic aneurysm. They'd rushed her to Theatre but he hadn't been able to stem the haemorrhage.

Her death had been a professional loss—not a personal one. He hadn't known the woman. He hadn't eaten home-made rhubarb tartlets from her family recipe. He hadn't met her husband. Telling him had been as awful as it always was, but his scheduled theatre list had been severely disrupted because of the emergency and he'd still had three more patients to deal with so the death had been quickly filed under 'Impossible save', as triple As too often were.

'Why don't I drop by on Saturday and see them? I'm on call so—'

'Oh, would you?' she interrupted, her voice charged with hope.

'Of course.'

Her exhalation was noisy in the confines of the car. 'Thank you,' she said, glancing at him quickly before returning her attention to the road.

Callum's night vision might be rubbish but he could still see the shine of unshed tears in her eyes. He'd never met a woman who wore her emotions so openly. Once upon a time that would have made him want to run as far away as possible.

Tonight it made him want to pull her closer.

Felicity was still stewing over the word *lovely* when they arrived at the art show. She shouldn't be. Callum's offer to see Mrs Dunnich should be dominating her thoughts and she should still be grateful for that but somehow his *lovely* resonated the most.

Now she understood his dismay that day when she'd described their time on the train as lovely. It was such an... insipid word.

It shouldn't bother her. They were *friends* and attracting Callum wasn't her aim.

Absolutely not.

She'd worn the dress for *herself.* Because she didn't get the opportunity to dress up very often and everyone else would be making the effort. Because she was single and one day she hoped not to be—Mr Right *could* be in Drayton's Crossing. Because rocking a little black dress was a marvellous thing and putting one on one of life's great joys. Like sexy lingerie and expensive chocolate.

She'd worn the dress for herself, damn it.

But then Callum had said 'lovely' and she'd realised she might have possibly, somewhere deep in her subconscious, worn it for him...

'There's Bill and Angela,' Callum said, his hand at her elbow.

Felicity looked around the transformed space. It had Veronica's artistic signature all over. Gone was the quaint hundred-year-old farmers' hall and in its place was a high-class bordello. Hundreds of metres of rich burgundy velvet were draped artfully overhead and lined the walls to form a dramatic backdrop to the paintings. There was a heavy reliance on gold brocade, plush velvet chaises and art deco standing lamps covered with red chiffon shawls to create a seductive pink glow.

Curvy women dressed in corsets and fishnet circulated with trays of champagne and canapés amongst the crowd milling around the paintings.

It was hard to believe this was little old Drayton's Crossing. It could be in any posh city gallery anywhere in the world, and while she knew about three-quarters of the peo-

ple in the room, there were certainly some she didn't rec-
ognise. Probably from Adelaide. Veronica's art was highly
sought after and her exhibitions, regardless of location, were
always well attended.

'You want champagne?'

The fine hairs on Felicity's nape prickled as Callum's
voice, low and close to her ear to be heard over the noise,
did funny things to her equilibrium. She was conscious of
his presence behind her. His bulk, his heat, the waft of his
citrusy aftershave. The warmth of his breath on her temple.

Her eyelids fluttered closed, she swayed a little as she
fought the urge to lean back. Let herself drape against him.

And wouldn't *that* just give everybody something more
to gossip about?

They weren't in a city gallery somewhere. They were in
Drayton's Crossing, for Pete's sake.

Felicity locked her quads and cleared her throat. 'Yes,
please.' Anything to remove the temptation of him from her
orbit long enough to get back some control.

'Be right back,' he murmured. 'Don't go away.'

Not much chance of that with legs as useless as two wet
noodles.

She watched him go. Somehow he seemed more hip,
cool, stylish and sexy than any other guy in the room—even
the arty types who clearly weren't from these parts. He was
wearing a suit the colour of roasted Arabica beans that he'd
teamed with a purple shirt, left open at the neck. No tie.

He looked the ultimate in casual, urban chic. And the
way those trousers pulled across his butt as he walked away
should be utterly illegal.

There was nothing *lovely* about it.

By the time he came back, Felicity was talking to an old
friend from Vickers Hill and she was on much more steady
ground. In fact, for the rest of the night, as they went from
painting to painting, there was always someone she knew,

someone to introduce Callum to and mingle with to prevent them from being alone.

Because they needed to avoid that at all costs. She wasn't stupid, she could tell people were openly curious, watching them and their every move. It was why she tried extra hard to project a friendly, collegial discourse between them.

She was careful about her stance and other nonverbal cues, she kept the conversation about the paintings and suppressed the urge to touch him, which was surprisingly difficult. She'd never realised how tactile she was in conversation until she had to physically stop herself a dozen times from touching Callum's arm.

She seriously deserved an award for her portrayal of *just-friends-nothing-to-see-here-move-along-please.*

Finally, she got to introduce him to Veronica. Felicity had been trying to get to her all night but her friend had been swamped with both buyers and well-wishers.

'V.,' Felicity said with a smile as her friend enveloped her in an enthusiastic, champagne-slopping hug. 'This is fabulous. You must be so pleased.'

'Absolutely thrilled, darl.' Big hoop earrings matched wild brown curls and the whole kaftan-alternative vibe Veronica had going on. Not for the first time, Felicity wished she oozed the same brash sexiness that was like a second skin for Veronica.

'I've sold just about every painting. Reckon the Clare Valley fire service will get about fifty k out of their cut by the end of the night.'

'That's amazing. They'll be giving you the keys to the valley next time you're home,' Felicity teased.

One of the things she most loved about Veronica was that she hadn't lost her connection with her roots. Her artwork may be hung in galleries around the world but at heart she was a small-town girl.

'As long as they're able to open every cellar door in the district then I'm fine with that.' Veronica laughed in her disarmingly self-deprecating way before turning her attention to Callum. 'Well, hello, there,' she said, as Felicity took a nervous sip of her remaining champers. 'So *you're* the guy she's doing.'

Felicity almost inhaled her drink at the outrageous statement. 'V.,' Felicity warned, coughing and spluttering on the bubbles that had almost gone down the wrong way as Callum threw back his head and laughed, seemingly unconcerned.

'What?' Veronica asked with a faux aura of innocence. 'All I was going to say is I approve, darling.' She eyed Callum up and down. 'If you've got to be in trouble with the town, might as well make it worth your while.' She held her hand out to Callum. 'Hi, I'm V.'

'Callum.'

'Callum, huh?' Veronica shook her head. 'You look like a Cal to me.'

Callum grinned and Felicity wanted to stomp on his foot. 'I get that as well.'

'I *bet* you do, darl.' Veronica laughed, tapping his shoulder lightly. She switched her attention to Felicity. 'He's good in bed, right? I can just tell.'

Felicity glanced around, hoping nobody was eavesdropping. She'd forgotten how outrageous Veronica could be. She had no filter and lived to scandalise.

'I am not doing him.' Felicity hissed, while Callum— *Cal*—chuckled some more. Which *was* true. *Currently*, she wasn't. 'The gossips have got it wrong as usual.'

'Well, you should make it right,' Veronica murmured, her gaze eating Callum up again. 'If you can't beat them, darling, you might as well join them.'

Felicity was beginning to regret introducing them. Veronica's attention was a little too lascivious for her liking as a spike of something that felt very much like jealousy prodded Felicity in the chest.

Thankfully she noticed a couple heading their way with an artistic fever in their eyes, clearly intent on monopolising the *artiste* for as long as Veronica was willing to put up with them. 'Oh, look,' Felicity said, tipping her chin at the approaching zealots, 'Buyers incoming. Don't let us keep you.'

She shot her insanely vibrant and attractive friend a sweet smile as she seized Callum's arm and pulled him away. Veronica laughed, clearly neither fooled nor insulted, blowing a couple of quick air kisses before turning her attention on her fans.

They ended up in a corner, near a standing lamp emanating a very distracting pink glow. The crowd had thinned slightly, which enabled them to have a little more privacy.

Not that that had been the objective.

She had no idea what to say to Callum after Veronica's directness. At least everyone else had been discreet about their curiosity. She slugged back the dregs of her champers and immediately wished she could swig another. But as she was driving she grabbed a soda water off a passing tray instead. Callum snagged a beer.

Felicity sipped and wondered whether she should mention Veronica at all—apologise for her maybe. Explain she lived to scandalise. But frankly she was still too embarrassed to head down that track.

'V. seems like a hoot.'

Well. That was settled, then. Looked like they were going to talk about her whether she wanted to or not. 'She is. Sorry about that. She loves to shock people.'

He shook his head, tracking Veronica's movements. 'I think she's fabulous.'

Felicity nodded. Yes. He would. Veronica was probably much more his type than she was. She could imagine him back before his injury with someone delightfully brash and flirty like Veronica. Someone who was socially outgoing, confident in herself and her sexuality.

'She's gorgeous, isn't she? So out there and...' Felicity cleared her throat of the sudden husky stricture threatening to close it right off '...sexy.'

His head swivelled in Felicity's direction, one eyebrow cocked. 'Sexy, huh?'

Heat suffused her face as he studied her like he was seeing her through new eyes, his gaze drawing her in as if they were the only two people in the room. 'A woman can appreciate sexiness in another woman,' she said, a defensive streak in her voice a mile wide.

He held up his hands in mock surrender. 'I totally agree. It's a kinda sexy thing to admit, actually.'

So she was sexy now instead of lovely?

Heat flared between them. She suddenly wished they *were* the only two people in the room. The thought was nine parts thrilling, one part panic inducing. She couldn't afford to lose her head in front of all these people and lose all the 'just mates' groundwork she'd laid over the last hour or so.

'Who, me?' she murmured, keeping her voice low and silky. 'Impossible. I'm *lovely*, remember?'

'Ah.' He chuckled, his lips twitching on the rim of his glass before he took a mouthful of beer. 'Sorry about that. It was a bad word choice.'

'Oh, I don't know,' she said, the irritation from earlier returning with a vengeance as she mimicked what he'd said that day they'd visited Meryl. 'You could have said *nice*.'

He glanced around before his gaze drifted to her mouth. 'Trust me, it was cleaner than what I was really thinking.'

The low admission rumbled from his lips and stroked her in all the good places. She should just leave that alone. But some devil inside her wanted to know what he thought of her black dress.

'Oh?' She hoped the vibrato in her voice didn't betray how very badly she *needed* to know.

'It's not really for...' he looked around again before returning his gaze to hers, lowering his head and leaning in slightly as his voice went down a register '...polite company.'

Felicity was beyond caring about polite as his warm breath stirred the wisps of hair at her temple. A wave of goose-bumps swept down the side of her face and fanned out across her neck. She swayed closer, as if he was pulling her with an invisible thread, locking them in a private little bubble amidst all the colour and movement around them.

'Maybe you should whisper it?' she suggested, turning her lips towards his ear, her voice almost as low and rough as his. She was thankful for her heels bringing their heights closer.

She swore she could *feel* his smile as he leaned in to do just that, his lips brushing her hair.

Felicity's breath hitched and something deep and low clenched down hard as he whispered a very dirty word. It wasn't Shakespeare. It was bald and base and primal.

Such a freaking turn-on.

'And for what it's worth,' he muttered, pulling back so he could stare into her eyes, '*you* are the sexiest woman in the room tonight.'

Felicity swallowed as her legs threatened to melt to jelly again and land her on her butt.

'*Ah*. Here you are!' Angela said, sliding an arm around Felicity's waist, seemingly oblivious to the mood. 'Cal, I need to borrow Flick for a moment. Someone has to come with me while I pay for my painting and stop me from buying another one. She's disciplined like that.'

Felicity didn't get a chance to refuse as Angela dragged her away, but she did glance over her shoulder to find Callum had her firmly in his sights, carnal intent blazing from his eyes.

How they were going to get home without pulling over and jumping each other's bones she had no idea.

CHAPTER ELEVEN

THEY LEFT AN hour later. An hour during which Felicity spent as much time *away* from Callum as possible, mingling with other people as she fought to get her body back under control. Because, while it was clear now that their sexual attraction was never going to allow them to be the friends she'd hoped they could be, it didn't mean succumbing to their attraction was the right thing either.

There was no point getting close to him when it would be *her* heart bruised in the end. Sure, she could have a fling with him but the truth was she'd never been good at casual sex.

Feelings always came in to it for her. Not necessarily love but a very definite connection. That's just the way she was.

It was like a reverse superpower. Her kryptonite. It made her weak.

Before Ned she'd had three serious relationships. Two had lasted six months. One had lasted nine. She was an emotional person—she liked to be invested and committed to the men she dated.

She liked being attached to another person.

But Callum was a different prospect. He'd already admitted to not forming attachments. To having a string of affairs with women during his darkest hours. And he was still coming to terms with a lot of baggage.

It didn't take a brain surgeon to figure out she'd be the more invested of the two of them if she let this thing become more than what had happened on the train. And in her car. And here tonight. She already liked him way more than was wise, especially now he'd proved to be a halfway decent doctor as well.

And then where would she be? Vickers Hill had always felt safe to her. It was her home, the place she'd run to after Ned. The place where she'd come into her own and found her feet. She didn't want to have to run from it as well because it was too painful to stay.

So she wasn't going to go there. But…she was Callum's lift home so she had to find some way to reboot the direction of the night. Maybe her overwhelming desire to have sex with him *was* going to get in the way of a friendship but that didn't mean she couldn't be friendly.

And for that she had to steer the conversation. Because she had no doubt if she steered it the wrong way, Callum would merrily follow.

'Tell me about your brother,' she blurted out as she pulled out of the car park, hyper-aware of the intimacy created by the glow of the dashboard lights and the slow ballad playing on the radio. 'Sebastian, right?'

Callum frowned, obviously not expecting that after the tension that had been building between them. 'Seb,' he corrected. '*That's* what you want to talk about?'

Felicity did not take her eyes off the road. 'That's what I want to talk about.'

He didn't answer for long moments and Felicity held her breath. Was he going to call her on it? Was he going to slip his hand on her leg and turn her into putty?

Everything seemed to hang in the balance as the seconds stretched. Then he sighed and said, 'What do you want to know?'

She shrugged, gripping the steering wheel hard as relief coursed through her system. 'Everything, I guess. He is living with our Luci after all. I'm pretty sure she hasn't told her parents yet so I feel like someone should at least know something about him.'

'In case he's a serial killer?'

Felicity ignored the derision. 'Exactly.'

'Anything specifically? "Everything" is kind of broad.'

'Is he older or younger than you?'

'Three years younger.'

'And he lives with you?'

'No. He doesn't live anywhere in particular, he just crashes at my place when he's in Sydney.'

Felicity frowned at the section of road lit up by her headlights, conscious of dry bushland flying by in her peripheral vision. Seb Hollingsworth—who was living with Luci—was some kind of...drifter?

'So he's...homeless?'

Callum's low chuckle enveloped her, wrapping her up, reminding her how alone they were. Not that being surrounded by people had seemed to matter back at the art show either.

'No. He has a boat that he's doing up with plans to live on it, eventually.'

'Does he have a job to support that plan?' A thirty-one-year-old guy with no fixed abode wasn't exactly inspiring confidence.

'Yes.' Callum chuckled again. 'He's a community health physician, employed by the government. He travels around a lot, mainly in rural areas.'

'Which is why he doesn't have his own place?'

'Yes. That and the fact he's allergic to putting down roots ever since his pregnant girlfriend was killed in a hit-and-run accident a few years back.'

Felicity blanched at the casual imparting of such a tragic tale, flicking a quick glance at him before returning it to the road. The awful news socked her right in the centre of her chest and tears pricked her eyes. 'Oh, God.' She absently patted her chest. 'How *awful* for him.'

'Yes. It was a terrible time. He kind of changed after that. Moved in a completely different direction. Sold their house, bought a motorbike and a run-down boat and started working away a lot.'

Felicity had no doubt something like that could irrevocably change a person. It seemed like both the Hollingsworth men were good at running away. 'Sounds like he's a bit of a wherever-I-lay-my-hat kinda guy.'

'Yeah,' he agreed. 'I think that sums him up perfectly.'

'Are you close?'

Right from the beginning, Callum had come across as utterly self-contained. It was hard to reconcile him having a sibling. If she'd been forced to guess she would have said he was an only child.

He shrugged. 'We're not bosom buddies. But we have a solid relationship built on mutual respect for us both needing our own space.'

Well…that was suitably vague… And sad. It seemed to her that the Hollingsworth brothers could have been a great support to each other during their respective tragedies if they'd come together instead of running away.

But, then, what did she know about sibling relationships? She *was* an only child.

'So,' he said, interrupting her thoughts, 'does Seb pass muster now he has a tragic backstory?'

He was teasing but Felicity didn't see the funny side. 'I don't think it's something you should be making light of,' she chided, aware that she probably sounded like some puritan but unable to easily shake off the lingering sadness of Seb's tragedy.

'Its fine.' He laughed. 'Every year for Christmas Seb sends me a brochure from the guide dogs society. We're blokes, we talk smack and joke about our problems, that's how we bond.'

Felicity rolled her eyes. *Men.* She'd always wanted a brother. Now she wasn't so sure. She wondered what Luci, fellow single child, nurse and sucker for a wounded man, was making of Seb.

'Well, does he or doesn't he?' Callum prompted.

Knowing more about Seb was comforting. She just hoped Luci's vagueness when she talked about him wasn't because she was falling for him. Luci was getting over a painful divorce and Seb Hollingsworth didn't sound like he was ready for a relationship.

Kind of like his brother.

'I'm not about to ring Luci and tell her to get out of the house.'

'Good.' He nodded. 'From what I can gather, she's fine with him being there anyway. And if she wasn't he'd have probably just crashed in the boat. Or, if he'd been absolutely desperate, at my parents' place.'

So Callum had parents in Sydney. 'They don't get on?'

He shrugged. 'Their relationship is a little...fraught.'

'They don't approve of his lifestyle?'

'They don't approve of his *career* choice. They're surgeons. In fact, *all* the Hollingsworths are surgeons,' he said, a core of something that sounded like bitterness infecting his voice. 'Seb chose something outside the field so he's always been a disappointment to them.'

Felicity couldn't begin to imagine her parents being disappointed in *anything* she'd chosen, let alone medicine. The son of a train driver and the daughter of a dairy farmer had only ever wanted happiness for their child. They'd retired to the coast now but were thrilled that Felicity had found her niche in life.

'They must be very proud of you, carrying on the family tradition?' she observed.

'They *were.*'

'Were?' She sneaked a peek at his face, his profile contorting into a grimace, before she looked back at the road.

Surely they'd supported him during and after his injury?

'They think I've given up a little too easily.'

Felicity touched his arm without thinking, just as she would have done to anyone to express her empathy. 'I'm sorry.' No wonder Callum and Seb ran away from their stuff when there was no one for them to run *to.*

'It's fine,' he dismissed, with a shrug, dislodging her

hand. 'I'm used to their indifference. We both are. They're just not cut out to be parents. Some people aren't.'

'But still…' She couldn't wrap her head around it.

'It's fine,' he repeated. 'Don't feel sorry for me. Seb and I grew up with a lot of privilege that many of the kids around us didn't. We didn't want for anything.'

Materialistically, maybe not, but Felicity didn't have to be a psychologist to know what kids needed most were engaged, interested, supportive parents.

'And I think we turned out kinda okay despite them. Well…' he shot her a lopsided grin '…*I* did at least. The jury's still out on Seb.'

Her mouth twitched. Callum Hollingsworth in full charm mode was a force to be reckoned with and she didn't have it in her after such serious subject matter to deny him a little lightness. 'Yeah,' she murmured, sneaking him another look. 'You're kinda okay.'

He grinned at her for a beat or two. Felicity's pulse fluttered and her breath hitched as the moment stretched. She broke it by looking back at the road and the far reach of the headlights illuminating the ghostly white trunks of gum trees.

He didn't say anything for a while and the music filled the space between them. 'About before…' he said eventually.

'No.' Felicity shook her head. 'Let's not do this. Let's mark it up to champagne and vanity and never talk about it again. Okay?'

She held her breath, waiting for his agreement. What she'd do if he didn't, she had no idea. If he looked at her and said *Screw that*, what *would* she do? Probably pull the car over and do him on the side of the road.

'We seem to do that a lot,' he said after a silence that was loud enough to obliterate the music. 'Avoid talking about this thing between us. I'm not sure it's very healthy.'

'No.' Felicity shook her head again vigorously. 'Un-

healthy would be flat-out denial. I'm not denying it. I'm
ignoring it.'

'And by *it* you mean our red-hot sexual attraction?'

Felicity's fingers tightened around the wheel at Callum's
unnecessary summation. 'Yes,' she muttered.

As if she needed any reminding.

'That. But you and I are *not* going there. So there's no
point talking about what happened before because nothing happened.'

The fact he'd turned her on in a crowded room with just
one, dirty, whispered word didn't count.

He gave a short, sharp laugh. 'Now, *that's* denial.'

Yeah. He had her there. But she only had two options and
pulling the car over and having him prove that word to her
wasn't a viable one. So she had to forge ahead.

With conversation.

Or turn the music up really loud and not talk at all.

She chose the latter.

Callum was still thinking about that trip home on Thursday
night and their awkward goodbye when he dialled Felicity's
number on Saturday morning from the Dunnich garden. It
was a walk in the park compared to what he was about to
tell her. He'd put up with a dozen awkward goodbyes in ex-
change for this one sad hello.

'Hey,' she said, her voice perky.

She'd used that tone of voice with him all day yesterday.
Perky. So damn cheerful. It had been amusing then but it
grated this morning.

He'd never met a woman so determined to keep him at
arm's length.

'What's up?'

For a moment he didn't want to tell her. He just wanted
to soak up the November sun beating down on his neck
and get lost in the heady aroma of roses and the lazy drone
of bees, knowing she was in his ear, breathing and perky.

'Callum?' she prompted, some of the perkiness dissolving.

His heart punched the centre of his chest with slow, precise jabs as he took a steadying breath. 'I'm at Alf's.'

There was a pause on the end of the line, a pause that was so damn loud he could practically hear every thought careening through her head. 'What's happened?'

Her voice was low, serious, resigned. All the perkiness was gone. It was matter-of-fact now. Professional. But he could also hear the slight huskiness. Could picture her big grey eyes growing bright.

'It's Lizzy.' Callum looked over his shoulder to the open back door. He could see Alf's silhouette as he talked on the phone in the central hallway. 'She's had a massive stroke.'

No pause this time, no grilling him for the details. Just, 'I'll be right there', and the phone going dead.

Callum put his phone in his back pocket and went inside, the cool and relative darkness a stark contrast to the bright morning outside. He pushed his sunnies on top of his head and headed for Alf, who hung up the landline as he neared.

'That was our daughter in Adelaide,' he said, his usually strong, slow drawl weak and tremulous as he stared at the device. 'She's going to let everyone know and then head up to us.' He glanced at Callum. 'Do you think she'll h…?' His voice wobbled and cracked. 'Hold on till then, Doc?'

Callum was surprised Lizzy had even lasted this long. Her breathing was affected by the stroke. It had improved since he'd placed some nasal prongs on and run in a trickle of oxygen but Callum didn't think she'd see out too many more hours.

He slid his hand on Alf's shoulder and gave a squeeze. 'I reckon she will, Alf.' Because he needed hope now more than anything.

He nodded, his lips trembling, suddenly looking every one of his eighty-plus years. 'Did you get hold of Flick?' he asked gruffly.

'Yes. She should be here shortly.'

'Rightio,' Alf said, staring at the door to his bedroom and straightening his shoulders as if he was going into battle. How did a husband say goodbye to a wife he'd been with for almost seventy years? 'I'm going back in.'

Callum nodded and wished he didn't feel so out of his depth. He hadn't done this in a long time—stood by and done nothing while a patient slowly slipped away.

He was used to action. To *saving* people.

But Alf had been adamant after Callum had diagnosed the stroke that Lizzy not go to hospital and produced an advance care directive that stated Lizzy didn't want any extraordinary measures taken to save or prolong her life in the event of another major stroke.

'She wants to be here with her family and Bailey by her side,' he'd said.

And Callum understood that, he just didn't know what Alf needed of him right now. It felt wrong to be witnessing something so intimate when he barely knew them. It felt like an intrusion. But he knew he couldn't leave Alf either.

It was why he'd suggested Felicity come and sit with Alf until his family arrived and the old man had jumped at the idea.

'Can I bring you in a cup of tea or something?'

'No, thanks, Doc,' Alf said, and quietly slipped into the room.

A well of uselessness swamped him, familiar and over-whelming. He'd felt like this after the accident when the extent of his injury had sunk in. He'd hated it then and he hated it now.

He had to be able to do something, surely?

He wandered aimlessly to the open front door, pulling his sunglasses down as the brightness jabbed into his permanently dilated left pupil like a knife. He looked up and down the street, willing Felicity's car to arrive, for her to walk through the front gate.

She'd know what to do.

A mix of floral aromas tickled his senses as he waited and his gaze was drawn to the beauty of Alf's garden. It drifted to the arbour that arched over the gate and was covered in climbing roses, and he wondered if these were the ones that Lizzy liked so much. They were pretty, a champagne colour and smaller than the ones growing on individual bushes. Dainty and feminine. Very much like her.

An idea hit him then and he smiled as he strode back into the house and searched the kitchen for a pair of scissors. Maybe filling her room with the aroma of her beloved roses could be his contribution?

Who knew what she could still hear, see and smell?

Locating some scissors in a drawer, he headed back out, stopping at the first bush near the front porch and snipping one of the blooms. The front path was lined with bushes and as he had no real idea what he was doing, apart from avoiding the thorns, he figured he might as well snip one from each. Clearly arranging flowers wasn't his forte but they didn't need to be pretty—they just needed to provide some joy and, hopefully, some peace.

For Alf as well as Lizzy.

He was halfway through when Felicity pulled up. The surge of relief that flooded his chest flowed cool and electric through his veins.

'Hi,' she said as she pushed open the gate and walked under the arbour.

'Hi.' She was in strappy sandals, denim shorts that came to just above her knee and a tank top. She was Flick and she was exactly who he needed. 'I'm sorry for calling you for this—'

She shook her head, interrupting his apology, her loose ponytail brushing back and forth between her shoulder blades. 'You did the right thing. Is she…?'

'No,' he assured her quickly, and her shoulders visibly relaxed. 'She's unconscious but hanging on. Alf's family are driving up from Adelaide. I thought he needed a familiar face to wait with him until they got here.'

'Of course.' She gave him a sad smile, her expression full of empathy. 'What happened?'

'We were all chatting out in the back garden. Alf and I left Lizzy and Bailey there, watching a couple of the magpies they feed frolicking in the sprinkler, so he could take me in and show me some of his wines. We'd been gone a couple of minutes when Bailey started to bark.' Callum wiped the sweat off his brow with the back of his hand. 'Alf knew straight away. When we got to her she was slumped in the wheelchair, unconscious.'

'Oh, no,' she murmured. 'Poor Mr Dunnich.'

'He's been really good. Stoic, you know?' Callum had no idea how long it would last.

'Yes, he's country down to his bootstraps. And what about you?' she asked, peering at him hard as if she was trying to see behind his dark shades. 'Are *you* okay?'

The question surprised him. No colleague had ever asked him if he was okay over a work situation. Sometimes things went wrong and you just got on with it.

But, as he'd learned over the last three weeks, that wasn't the way they did things in Vickers Hill.

'Yes. Thanks.' It felt surprisingly good to have been asked. He may not have known the Dunniches for long but he'd been incredibly moved by Alf's gentleness as he'd laid Lizzy on the bed and stroked her hair. 'Better now you're here.'

Maybe that was one of the things he wasn't allowed to say but it was true. And not in a *hey, baby* way. In a *human* way. She knew Alf and Lizzy and she knew him.

They were all connected.

She glanced at the scissors in his hands and the stems he'd already picked. 'I didn't know what else to do,' he said. 'All I really know about her is how much she loves roses so I figured…'

Overly bright eyes smiled at him. 'I think that's a really beautiful thing to do. Lizzy would love that.'

Callum's chest swelled. He'd felt like a clumsy fool with his black thumb cutting pretty roses in someone else's garden—completely conspicuous. But Felicity's compliment validated his instincts.

'You can leave them in the kitchen if you want. I'll find a vase for them in a bit.'

'I can do it,' Callum dismissed.

A tiny frown caused a little V between her brows. 'Oh… okay, sure. Thanks.'

It was Callum's turn to frown. She didn't sound so sure and he certainly didn't know the etiquette here. 'Is it? Okay?'

'Of course. I just…didn't think you'd want to stick around. You don't have to, you know. I've got this.'

She was letting him off the hook. Three weeks ago Callum would have taken that offer and run with it. Left the nurse to deal with relatives and the patient comfort stuff.

But he wasn't that person any more. *Thanks to her.*

'I'd like to stay…if you don't think it's intruding.'

'That would be great,' she said, her smile gentle, her hand sliding onto his arm and giving it a pat.

Callum glanced at it, surprised at how comforting it was. 'Is she in the bedroom?' He nodded and she edged around him, her hand dropping away. 'I'll see you in there,' she murmured.

He watched her disappear inside the house, the imprint of her hand still marking his skin. Kind of like the way she'd marked his life. In just a few short weeks the girl from the train had taught him more about himself than he'd learned in thirty-plus years. More about being a doctor. More about the things that actually mattered.

Whatever did or didn't happen between them he knew one thing for sure—he was *never* going to forget Felicity Mitchell.

* * *

Callum stepped into the room fifteen minutes later. He'd found a vase under the sink and arranged the blooms. It was never going to win a floral arrangement competition but it wasn't bad for his first time.

He placed them on an old-fashioned dressing table.

'Thanks, Doc,' Alf said. He was sitting on a chair beside the bed, holding his wife's hand. Felicity was sitting next to Alf, holding his hand. 'Lizzy loves her roses, don't you, darlin'?' he asked, patting her hand a couple of times.

'Do you remember that time Bailey dug up those new bushes she'd planted when he was a puppy?' Felicity asked. 'And how hard Bailey worked to get back into her good graces.'

Alf chuckled. Bailey, who was lying on the bed with Lizzy, whined and thumped his tail at the mention of his name but he didn't move his head from Lizzy's thigh.

Callum listened for the next couple of hours as Alf regaled them with stories about Lizzy and their life together. There was so much humour and love in every one but Alf's voice often cracked and Callum could only guess how hard it was for him to watch his beloved wife slipping away.

Her respirations changed as they chatted in the bedroom and by the time the first family members arrived Lizzy's breathing had slowed right down. There were more due to arrive over the course of the afternoon and Alf was praying that everyone could get here before the end, but deep down Callum didn't hold out much hope.

Callum and Felicity moved out to the kitchen to give the family time together. They didn't really talk much, just kept busy, making cups of tea and coffee and refilling them as often as required. At lunchtime Callum went out and bought some loaves of bread and sandwich fillers, which they turned into a couple of crammed platters, and later, for afternoon tea, they were able to rustle up enough home cooking to satisfy everyone.

By the time Lizzy took her last breath at four o'clock, all the family that could be there were by her side. Callum marvelled at her staying power. He had clearly underestimated Alf's wife. It was as if she'd been hanging on for all her family before passing away.

They were washing up when Bailey howled. All the hairs on Callum's nape stood on end. Felicity's hands in the hot, sudsy water stilled. He waited for her to say something but she didn't, she just stood in silence for long moments. He wasn't sure what he should do but he wanted to do *something*. To give her some comfort. He knew how close she was to Alf and Lizzy but she'd held herself together today. He'd seen how hard it had been, seen her rapid blinking on more than one occasion as she'd comforted an upset Alf.

Tentatively, he slid an arm around her shoulders. She was stiff, like she might shatter into a thousand pieces, and for a moment he thought she was going to stay like that until he murmured, 'I'm sorry.' Then her shoulders suddenly slumped and her body leaned against his, her head resting on his biceps.

He dropped a kiss on her honey-blonde hair and they stayed there for a long time as he gently rubbed his hand up and down her arm.

A part of him wished he could do more but this, doing nothing, was somehow so much more intimate.

It felt right.

CHAPTER TWELVE

FELICITY STARED OUT of the window of Callum's car as he pulled up in front of her place and cut the engine. She'd offered to leave her car at Alf's so the large extended family had an extra car to get around in the next few days, which had left Callum to drive her home.

It was seven in the evening and the shadows of the gum trees in her front yard were just starting to lengthen. She and Callum had stuck around and notified all the right people and made the arrangements for Lizzy to be taken away. She'd wanted to free Alf and his family from the burden of it all so they could just grieve and hold each other.

Alf's 'I don't know what I'm going to do without her, Flick' ran on a continuous loop through her head. His devastation had reached inside her and squeezed her gut and still weighed heavily against her chest.

'We need to keep an eye on Alf the next little while,' she said. Felicity hadn't even registered the silence in the car until she broke it.

'You don't think he'd try to...'

Felicity shook her head, her gaze fixed on the shadows outside the car. 'No. But they've been together a lot of years. It wouldn't be the first time a spouse had died close on the heels of a long-term partner.'

'Good point.'

'I'll organise some community health services,' she said, her brain flipping through the options. 'And I'll mobilise the Country Women's Association.'

Felicity knew the CWA would rally around Alf. Lizzy

had been the local president for about twenty years—Alf would never have to cook again.

'His daughter said quite a few of them were sticking around until after the funeral and she was going to stay on until Christmas. Apparently they're all going to spend it here with Alf.'

Christmas. It was hard to believe it was only five weeks away. 'That's good.'

They lapsed into silence again. Felicity looked at her house. It seemed so quiet and empty after the fullness of Alf's house today. She had never minded the quietness. It had been one of the joys of moving back to Vickers Hill after living in an apartment on a busy main road in Adelaide. But she didn't want to face the quietness now. She didn't want to be alone.

She turned her head to look at him. 'You want to come in for a drink?'

To say he looked taken aback by the offer was an understatement. 'There…seem to be a lot of reasons why I shouldn't.'

Felicity nodded. There were. But.

'I need a drink. A big one. And I don't want to be alone right now.'

His eyes searched hers for a beat or two. She wasn't sure what he was looking for but he must have been satisfied because he reached for the release button on his seat belt. 'I could definitely go a drink.'

Felicity was thankful as she unlocked her front door and Callum followed her into the house that she had no Mrs Smiths to worry about. Sure, people gossiped in her street too—where didn't they?—but her neighbours were mostly families, young mums too busy just getting through the day to worry about what Felicity was doing in the privacy of her own home.

'You were so good with Alf's family today,' he said from behind her as he followed her into her formal lounge room.

'Well, I've had plenty of practice,' she said as she poured them both a slug of her favourite whisky.

'Sure. I just figured you'd be...'

Felicity smiled to herself as she screwed the lid back on the bottle then turned, handing him his whisky. 'An emotional wreck? A blubbering mess?'

'I was thinking more along the lines of not quite so contained.'

She smiled again. Callum was treading carefully. 'Lizzy's death isn't about me and my feelings. It's about them. Her family. Me bursting into tears because *I'm* sad doesn't prioritise their grief and also puts the onus on them to comfort *me* during a time when they should only be thinking of themselves. It's selfish. Not helpful.'

'So you just...don't?'

'That's right.' She nodded. 'You just suck it up. Come home, have a drink and a long cry in the shower.'

Felicity looked into the depths of the amber fluid. The tears that had been threatening since she'd got the phone call this morning pushed closer to the surface. She blinked hard, swirled the whisky around the glass a few times before raising it towards him.

'To Lizzy.'

He tapped his glass against hers. 'To Lizzy.'

Felicity slugged back half of hers, sucking in a breath as the whisky burned all the way down. '*You* were pretty great too today,' she mused as she watched him over the rim of her glass.

He smiled. 'I had a good teacher.'

Felicity laughed. A short, sharp sound that was more wounded than joyous. It hurt. Deep inside her chest where it had been hurting all day.

He frowned and took a step towards her. 'Are you okay?'

'Nope.' Her voice wobbled, her smile wobbled. Everything wobbled inside as the soft concern in his voice undid her. 'But I will be tomorrow.'

A tear escaped. And then another.

'Felicity,' he whispered, placing his drink down on a nearby table and taking the step that separated them, his hands on her hips. 'Don't cry.'

She didn't want to, not in front of him, but crying came as naturally to Felicity as laughing. She'd thought the tears would hold off until she was alone. She was wrong.

'Sorry,' she said, embarrassed, dashing them away with her hands.

'Don't,' he said. 'Don't ever apologise for being who you are.'

It didn't help. The tears came faster.

'Hey,' he murmured, taking her glass and discarding it too before sliding his hands up her back, urging her against him.

Felicity went, shutting her eyes and bunching her fingers in his T-shirt, letting the tears fall. It was beyond her power to stop them.

'I'm sorry,' she repeated, the even thud of his heart comforting beneath her ear.

'Shh,' he said, his chin resting on top of her head. 'It's okay.'

It certainly felt okay, standing in the circle of his arms, weeping quietly. Losing Lizzy had taken a little chink out of her soul, as had every patient she'd ever lost. It was inevitable for someone like her whose emotions were barely skin deep, but having Callum here with her helped.

She glanced up at him. She was close enough to his neck to see every individual whisker, to press her nose to his throat and inhale the citrus essence of him. Fill herself up with that instead of the echoes of Alf finally breaking down and whispering, 'My darling, my darling, my darling', like his heart was shattering.

She angled her head back until she was looking into his eyes, eyes that told their own story of loss right there for the whole world to see.

'Thank you,' she said, rising up on tiptoe and kissing him.

For being here. For being *there*. For being better. For being what she needed exactly when she needed it.

Like right now.

He eyed her warily as he pulled back, his hands moving to her hips and pushing her away gently. But Felicity held firm. The night stretched ahead of her and she didn't want to be alone for any of it.

'Felicity?' His hands branded her hips as his confused eyes searched hers. Was he trying to find some kind of meaning as to why she'd kissed him? 'I'm not sure we should be doing this.'

Felicity was very sure they *shouldn't* be but she wanted it anyway. And the accelerated thud of his heart beneath her palm told her maybe he did too.

'I didn't mean this to be—' He stopped abruptly, obviously finding the right words difficult. 'I was just…trying to comfort you.'

'I know.' She did. And she appreciated it.

But…

She raised her hand, tracing her fingers along his jaw and up the side of his face. 'I just need a different kind of comfort tonight.'

He stared at her for long moments before covering her hand with his and bringing it to his mouth, dropping a kiss on her palm. It was such a gentle gesture Felicity's eyes welled with tears again.

His mouth lowered and he kissed her, soft and slow, like their very first kiss on the train before it had turned hot and heavy. The tears spilled over, trekking south, his thumbs wiping them away as he cupped her cheeks either side of her jaw, his gentleness so sweet she sighed his name against his mouth.

He eased away slightly. 'Take me to the nearest bed.'

The low, gravelly request slid right between her legs and,

without a word, Felicity took him by the hand and led him to her bedroom.

She turned as they crossed the threshold, seeing her bed in its usual unmade disarray. 'It's a little messy, I'm afraid I don't see the point in making my bed when—'

His mouth cut her off as his hands slid to her waist, bringing their bodies flush against each other. 'I don't care about mess,' he muttered, coming up for air, feathering kisses along her jaw to her ear. 'I just want to be inside you.'

Felicity's eyes fluttered closed. 'Oh, God,' she breathed, her hands on his shoulders. 'I want you inside me too.'

And then he was kissing her mouth again as he pulled at her tank top, peeling it off, and she was rucking up his T-shirt and hauling it over his head then reaching for the snaps on his shorts as he reached for hers, pushing them down his legs, kicking out of her own, their kissing stop-start as they shimmied out of their clothes.

Then they were naked and breathless and falling on the bed together in a tangle of limbs and impatience, and he was rolling her on her back, kissing down her neck to her breasts, sucking each nipple in turn, making her cry out and arch her back and forget everything about the day except this moment.

Nothing mattered right now but how they could make each other's bodies sing. Nothing mattered but him.

Her fingers tangled hard in his hair, holding him at her breasts, begging him for more. And he gave her more. More and more, his tongue taunting her until she saw stars. Until she was so damn wet and tingly and restless she was begging him to stop, begging him to finish it, to thrust himself inside her and take them both where they wanted to go.

Her nails dug into his back and she dragged his mouth off her nipple. 'I want you inside me.'

He kissed her hard before mumbling, 'Condom,' then heading back to torture her nipples some more.

Condom. *Right.* Bedside drawer.

Desperately she reached for it, crying out and arching her back when he resumed what he'd been doing, only the other side this time, his hard tongue circling and circling and circling until her eyes were rolling back in her head and her nipple was slippery and elongated, then sucking it deep into his mouth, his teeth scraping against the tip.

Her hand found a loose foil packet and she snatched it up, tearing it open as she pushed on his shoulder. 'Condom,' she panted.

He lifted his head and Felicity almost whimpered at the relief, the cool air stiffening her wet nipples into tight, hard cones. He grabbed the condom from her and shifted slightly to his side, sheathing himself in one deft move. Then she was reaching for him, grasping his shoulders, pulling him over her, spreading her legs wide so he could settle deep, reaching for his erection, exulting in his guttural groan as she squeezed all his glorious length, guiding him to where she was slick and needy.

'There,' she gasped as he nudged, thick and hard against her, tormenting her with the promise of his girth. 'Right there.'

'Oh, yeah,' he murmured, his voice a low growl. 'Right there.'

And then he was sliding home and she was calling out his name, wrapping her legs around his waist, asking him for more, feeling every hot, hard glide, shivering and shaking with each thrust, tilting her pelvis to meet each one, digging her fingers into his buttocks, revelling in the tremble through his thighs and biceps and the harsh suck of his breath as the friction built and the tension mounted, his arms hard bands of muscle bracketing her shoulders.

It wasn't long before the whole world started to unravel. A tiny ripple that started deep and low became two, then three. Then became stronger.

A contraction. Two. Three.

Then a shudder undulating along her pelvic floor.

Felicity gasped as the shudders escalated, increasing in intensity until she could barely stand it, her eyes flying open to find him watching her, their gazes locking in an intensely intimate moment.

The moment of mutual release.

'Yes,' he muttered, his brow crinkled in concentration, his biceps like granite in her peripheral vision, as his hips pumped faster and harder. 'I can feel you. I can feel you.'

Felicity cried out, fighting the urge to shut her eyes as she came, showing him all that she was as she flew apart. He joined her in the maelstrom moments later, his eyes wide open too, gifting her every second of his orgasm as it slammed through his body, the wonder and intensity of it reflected in his gaze until they were churned out the other end, sweaty, spent and utterly exhausted.

It was dark in her room but the red luminous figures on Felicity's bedside clock told her it was ten past one. She should be tired from the emotion of the day and the expended energy of the night. But she wasn't.

Callum was in her bed and while that was something she was going to have to deal with—*tomorrow*—she was going to enjoy it for the night. Like she had on the train.

She was tracing patterns on his chest as he stroked lazy fingers up and down her back. 'What do you see when you look at me?'

'Fishing for compliments?' Even rumbling through his chest wall straight into her ear, his voice didn't lose any of its amusement.

She smiled, her finger circling one flat, brown nipple. 'No. I'm being serious.'

His hand paused for a moment, missing a beat or two before continuing its steady pace. 'Okay. I see an incredible woman, a great lover and amazing nurse. I see—'

'No.' Felicity pushed off his chest, propping her head on her hand as she looked down at him, stroking a finger along his chin, under his bottom lip. 'I mean, what do you physically see? With your eye the way it is.'

He went very still. 'Oh. Right.'

Her finger paused on his chin. *Damn.* Way to kill the mood, Flick. 'I'm sorry. It's okay. I shouldn't have asked.'

Except lying here with him she'd realised she didn't know anything about the nitty-gritty of his eyesight. Mostly because he'd seemed so closed off about it but it seemed uncaring not to enquire.

Sure, it was easy to forget when looking at him that he had any kind of sight deficit. His misshapen, slightly dilated pupil and the fact he couldn't drive at night were the only indications. But it was hardly something *he* could forget. It wasn't like it was out of sight.

It *was* his sight.

'No. It's fine,' he assured her. 'You just took me by surprise, that's all. Nobody other than my specialists and the medical board have ever really asked.'

Felicity stroked her finger along his bottom lip. It was full and tempting. 'Didn't any of those women you shamelessly slept with after the accident ever ask?'

He smiled and she traced the curve of his mouth all the way to the corner and back again. 'They seemed more interested in bagging the blind surgeon than the details of my injury,' he said, his voice heavy with derision.

'Well, I'm interested,' she said, tapping his chin lightly.

'In the details or...' his hand slid onto her hip and lightly stroked '...bagging the blind dude?'

Felicity laughed, his tone light and more self-deprecating now. 'Huh. Been there, done that. Three times already tonight.'

His hand swept to her butt, scattering goose-bumps down the backs of her thighs and arrowing heat right between her legs. 'Fourth time's a charm.'

'Patience,' she teased, dropping a quick kiss on his mouth. 'Now, tell me how you see me.'

He sighed dramatically but kept up the drugging sweep of his hand from hip to buttocks and back again. 'At the moment, in the dark, not much with the left eye, you're kind of a dim blur.'

He was becoming a bit of a blur too as heat streaked to her pelvis. 'What about during the day? In normal light?'

'If I cover up my good eye, you'd be pretty blurred. The acuity in my left eye is shocking but my right eye compensates and if I'm wearing my glasses then the blurriness improves even further. But if you're standing on my left I probably wouldn't see you at all because my peripheral vision in that eye is pretty much nonexistent.'

The bitterness that had tinged his voice when he'd first told her about it was missing now. She wasn't sure if that was significant or just the result of three really good orgasms.

God knew, if she was any mellower at the moment from those orgasms and the very distracting stroke of his hand, she'd be floating away like a dandelion puff.

'They can't operate to help in any way?'

'They did what they could in the beginning. I've had quite a few surgical interventions, including laser work on my retina, but…frankly I don't think any of the specialists thought I'd have any kind of worthwhile vision so they're seeing it as a win.'

'And they think it's as good as it'll get?'

'It may improve marginally, in time but it's taken over two years to get where it is and most of that progress was made in the first year.'

'Are you still friends with the guy who bowled the ball?'

'Sure.' He shrugged. 'It's not his fault. It was a freak accident and I should have been wearing a helmet. I had one in my car but…'

Yeah. But…

Felicity was sure he'd done the should-haves and if-onlys over and over. It had been an expensive error in judgement and her heart went out to him. There was just something about this man that made her want to make it all better for him.

Enough bringing them down.

They had tonight and she was up for a little sexual healing.

'So, to recap,' she said, sliding her leg over and rolling up to straddle him, settling her slick heat over his semihardness, 'what you're saying is you see things right in front of you reasonably well in reasonable light, especially if you have glasses on.'

He chuckled, his hands moving to her hips. 'Yes.'

'So...' she arched her back, lifting the hair off her nape and piling it high on her head, two-handed '...it's not so good at the moment.'

'I can see enough,' he murmured, the heat from his gaze like an infra-red beam fanning over her breasts, prickling her nipples to tight, hard buds. 'And I have a pretty good imagination.'

'Would this help?' she asked, letting her hair go, leaning forward at the hips, reaching for the switch that was looped through the wrought-iron lattice of her bedhead.

She flicked it on and sat back to admire the effect of a dozen tiny fairy lights, embedded in plastic hearts woven through the metal, glowing soft and pink.

It was kind of how she felt now. Her heart on a string, all happy and glowy inside her.

'Oh, yes,' he muttered, his gaze zeroing in with laserlike intensity, his hands sliding up her sides.

His singular focus was an instant turn-on. 'Light not too harsh?' she teased.

He shook his head as his fingers stroked the undersides of her breasts. 'It's perfect.' He cupped them fully. 'You're perfect.' He brushed his thumbs across her aching nipples. 'So beautiful.'

Felicity moaned as his rapidly swelling erection pushed

hard against the knot of tingling nerves between her legs and she rubbed herself against him for maximum effect.

'God,' he groaned, vaulting upright, curling an arm around her waist and hauling her close. Felicity arched her back, offering her nipple to his questing mouth. She buried her hand in his hair, her eyes fluttering closed as his hot, wet mouth closed around her and she let herself get lost in the pleasure.

CHAPTER THIRTEEN

FELICITY WAS SITTING at the central island bench in her kitchen the next morning, reading the Sunday paper she had delivered to her door. A steaming-hot cup of coffee sat at her elbow as she tried to concentrate on some political scandal instead of the speech she had to give.

She'd heard the shower being turned on about fifteen minutes ago so it wouldn't be long now.

She'd been awake for a couple of hours, just watching him sleep, admiring the play of early morning shadows across his face and body. He looked so damn sexy in her bed.

When he was asleep. When he was awake. When he was thrusting into her, silhouetted by a fuzzy pink glow.

They would be memories she would treasure for ever.

But it couldn't be any more than another one-night stand. It would be too easy to spend the next five weeks in his arms and too hard to say goodbye. He wasn't ready. There were issues he still had to work out. And she didn't want to invest in someone who'd probably break her heart. It had taken her a long time to feel whole after Ned and she'd learned to be more guarded since then.

She just couldn't be the girl from the train here in Vickers Hill. She wasn't that reckless. Not in real life. Not with her reputation and not with her emotions.

'Good morning.'

The gravelly male voice coming from behind her ruffled all the tiny hairs on Felicity's nape. But there was wariness in his tone too. Was he feeling unsure after waking to an empty bed?

'Morning,' she said, not bothering to turn and acknowledge him, just slipping off her stool and heading for the percolator. 'Want a coffee?'

'Sure.' His tone was all wariness now.

She picked up a mug and poured him one, steeling herself to face him.

'Here you go,' she said, turning, mug in hand and a smile on her face. He was standing near the bench in his clothes from yesterday, except for his bare feet.

His hair was damp and he smelled like her shampoo.

Coconut had never smelled so damn good.

She slid his coffee across the bench, keen to keep something solid between them. 'Sit,' she said, leaning across to shift the newspaper out of the way.

Felicity didn't wait to see if he followed her command. She turned back to the percolator and poured herself another coffee. Her third for the morning. When she was done she made a beeline for the stool that was on her side of the bench and sat down, taking a sip of her drink.

He took one too and said, 'I feel like I'm about to get a "Dear John" speech.'

She shot him a nervous smile. 'Am I that obvious?'

He placed his mug on the countertop. 'Just say what you have to say, Felicity.'

She nodded. The direct approach was good. Rip that sticking plaster off and get on with it. 'Last night was...'

God, where did she even start with last night? The train had been good but last night had been better. It'd been emotional, not just sexual. A deeper connection born not just from what they'd shared yesterday but from three weeks of spending practically every day together.

And that scared the hell out of her.

'It's okay,' he said, his lips curling in a derisive smile. 'I think we can skip the compliments.'

'Okay.' She placed her mug down on the granite benchtop too. 'Last night was inevitable. It's been building for the last few weeks and after the train...well, I think we both know the train was never going to be enough when we've had to work together so closely.'

'*I* think if the next words that come out of your mouth are that you regret it or that *I* should regret it or that it was wrong or dumb or any other ridiculous statement then you should stop right there.'

Felicity gave a half-smile at his pre-emptive statement. His mouth was set in a hard line, his green eyes steely. He was even sexy when he was cranky. 'Nope.' She shook her head. 'No regrets.'

Never.

His mouth relaxed and his shoulders lost some of their tension. *Sexy, sexy, sexy.*

'But this can't become a regular thing,' she continued. 'I can't keep having sex with you and fooling myself that it's just some crazy interlude. Some mutual fun while you're here...that it'll all be okay. I'm just not built that way. I'm not the girl from the train. I was never really her. I'm just Flick from Vickers Hill.'

He didn't say anything for long moments, just stared at her as if he was trying to figure her out. 'Are you telling me...' he placed his bent elbow on the bench and supported his chin in his palm '...you don't even want to be friends?'

If only. Friends would make everything so much easier but that line was somewhere behind her now. 'I think I'm probably always going to want more than that from you.'

'Like...friends with benefits?'

She shook her head sadly. 'Like friends with *emotions*.'

Her admission sat him back, his arm dropping to the countertop. 'I see.'

She wondered if he did. Really did. 'You know what I thought last night when I turned those lights on? That that was me. That was my heart. Glowing all pink and beautiful inside my chest.'

He swallowed then, a light dawning in his eyes as the information slowly settled in. 'Are you trying to tell me that you're...?'

'No. I'm not,' she assured him. Quickly. Definitively. *She couldn't be.* It had taken her almost a year to realise she'd loved Ned. It would be preposterous to be in love with Callum after a few weeks. 'But...I *am* that kind of girl. Absence *doesn't* make my heart grow fonder. *Presence* makes it grow fonder and we can't keep doing this...' she waved her finger back and forth between them '...without...consequences. I *like* you, Callum.'

He was scheduled to leave on Christmas Eve and she was already sad about that day five weeks from now.

'I like you too.'

Felicity suppressed a snort. She didn't need to hear some quick-fire, city-slicker patronising response. He knew *exactly* what she meant. She folded her arms. 'A little *too* much.'

He dropped his gaze to his coffee as her point hit home and he fiddled with the handle. 'So we just...what?' he asked, glancing at her. 'See each other at work and that's it?'

'Yep.' Felicity nodded. 'Just colleagues...just two professionals. That's all.'

His gaze searched hers for what felt like an age, as if he was trying to assess just how serious she was. She didn't blink. Not once. Even though her hands were shaking around her mug and her pulse whooshed like a raging river through her ears.

'Okay. Sure. If that's what you want.'

Felicity nodded, amazed at her outer calm. 'It is.' Even though what she really wanted was for him to say, 'To hell with that,' pick her up and throw her down on her bed. The temptation to spend every night like last night almost overwhelmed her now she'd done herself out of the chance.

But he was going back to Sydney. He *had* to go back to Sydney. He had to work out what he wanted.

And living in a state of denial was preferable to living in a state of hope.

Two weeks later, in early December, Callum strode into the Parson's Nose—one of the many excellent gourmet pubs in town—searching the crowded room for his brother. If he'd been surprised to get a phone call from Seb—they had more of a texting relationship these days—he'd been utterly gobsmacked when Seb announced he was in Vickers Hill.

Today was Thursday, which was normally his day off, but Bill's brother had died a few days ago and the funeral was this morning so Callum had been covering for the old man. He hadn't minded and there had been the added bonus of seeing Felicity. But Bill had insisted he'd return for the afternoon appointments despite Callum encouraging him to take the whole day off.

Callum kept hearing from Julia about Bill retiring and all her grand plans for them but, as far as Callum could see, Bill wasn't ready to go yet. He certainly didn't seem to be in any hurry about finding a replacement.

'Cal!' Callum's head swivelled towards the voice and he squinted, trying to locate Seb. Finally he clocked his brother, waving and grinning, near the bar.

Callum made his way through several groups of people as Seb slid off his stool. When he finally reached the bar he pulled his brother in for a bear hug as they slapped each other on the back. The circumstances of their lives the last few years had meant a lot of separation but it was always good to see him again.

'Missing me, dude?' Callum said as they pulled apart.

'Always.' Seb laughed.

They settled on their bar stools and Seb waved the bartender over, ordering Callum a local beer. They watched as he poured then they clinked their glasses together and toasted brotherly love.

'What on earth brings you to sleepy little Vickers Hill?' Callum asked, swiping froth from his top lip.

'Well, it's not the surf.' Seb grinned.

Callum laughed. 'No. Definitely not.' He sighed. 'I *do* miss the surf.'

'Maybe I should be asking what on earth brings *you* to Vickers Hill?'

His brother may be younger but, being the black sheep of the family, he was never one for taking things at face value and always the one to ask probing questions. Even as a kid he'd wanted to know the whys, whats and where-fores of everything.

'I needed some…clear air.'

Seb regarded him over the rim of his beer glass for a beat or two. 'Have you found it?'

That was a much harder question to answer. Trust Seb to be the one asking it.

'Yes. And no.'

Seb lifted an eyebrow. 'Now, that requires further ex-planation so spill it, big brother.'

Callum didn't even know where to begin. In five weeks he *had* managed to find clear air regarding his career. He'd arrived here conflicted, hoping like crazy that a change in pace and scenery would enthuse him for his new path.

And it had.

He'd seen a different side to what had felt like the yoke of general practice and he'd been a better doctor out here then he'd been the last two years in any of his placements.

Thanks to Felicity.

Felicity…

Yeah. The air there was *far* from clear. Pretty damn murky, actually. She'd been strict about their interactions and things between the two of them had been exactly as she'd wanted. They saw each other at work from one p.m.

four days a week and rarely outside any more, apart from bumping into her at the shops or petrol station.

But that hadn't stopped the trip in his pulse whenever he heard her laughter or checking her out *every single time* she walked into the room. She'd been stringing tinsel up around the office all this week and she'd started wearing very distracting Christmas T-shirts and a red Santa hat with a cute white pom-pom on the end.

She seemed pretty damn cheerful, her easiness with him so effortless considering he had to check himself constantly. The urge to flirt, to slip into banter, to yank on that distracting white pom-pom was harder to suppress than he'd thought.

He had to keep reminding himself of what she'd said and who she was. She was a sensitive, empathic woman who'd taken him on to advocate for her patients and wasn't ashamed of how close her emotions bubbled to the surface. She'd got teary talking about her grandfather the first day he'd met her. Not to mention her reaction over Seb's fiancé and, of course, her tears for Lizzy Dunnich.

I'm that kind of girl.

That's what she'd said. And he was aware of it every day, watching her with the people she worked with and her patients. The way she cooed over the babies and clucked over the oldies, cheered over the wins and bossed the noncompliant with such a loving hand.

She *wasn't* like other women he'd met. She wasn't the kind he could play with and leave. Just walk away from and know she'd be okay. She'd told him she liked him. A woman had never told him she liked him. They'd confessed their love, their desire, their admiration. Their wildest sexual fantasies. But, looking back, he wasn't sure any of them had *liked* him.

And he'd never really told a woman he liked her either. In fact, he'd taken himself by complete surprise when he'd said it back. But it had felt right and he found himself not wanting to screw it up. To leave with her still liking him, even if it meant having to ignore his libido.

Because he *was* going back to Sydney.

He had to go back. He had a lot to prove.

'Uh-oh,' Seb said, waiting with a cocked eyebrow, clearly amused at Callum's prolonged contemplation. 'That bad?'

He glanced at his brother. 'There's this woman...'

'It's always a woman.' Seb chuckled.

Callum shook his head. 'Felicity isn't just any woman.'

'Felicity?' Seb frowned. 'Do you mean Flick? Luci's friend?'

'Yep.' And he told his brother everything.

'Well?' Callum asked after he'd run out of steam and his beer glass was empty.

'Well, what?'

'What do you think? Am I crazy?'

'Hell, Cal,' Seb groaned. 'Don't ask me. Luci has me so tied up in knots I don't know what to do any more either.'

'Luci?' It was Callum's turn to frown. '*My* Luci?'

'*Your* Luci?'

'I mean the one in my apartment?'

'Yes. She's the reason I'm here today. Her uncle died—'

'I know,' Callum interrupted. 'I've been covering the morning appointments for her father.'

With Felicity.

'Right. Well, she came back for the funeral and I know coming back and facing the town again was hard so...I thought I'd be here for her.'

'You *know*?'

Seb shrugged and, if Callum wasn't very much mistaken that was a smile breaking across his brother's face. 'We... talk. We've got close.'

Callum blinked. Could Seb actually be taking an interest in another woman after all this time? He hoped so. His brother had been to hell and back. 'Good for you. You've been through a lot, man. You deserve to be happy.'

Seb looked him straight in the eye. 'So do you, Cal. So do you.'

Callum appreciated the sentiment but his loss had been nothing compared to Seb's. 'Well,' he said, changing the subject, 'I'm sure Luci is very pleased to have you here.'

'Oh, she doesn't know yet. I only made up my mind this morning and jumped an early flight.' Seb checked his watch and quickly downed the dregs of his beer. 'So I'd better get going. The funeral should be over by now.'

He stood and Callum followed suit. They shook hands and shared another bear hug. Seb mumbled something about spending Christmas together and then he was striding out of the pub, his 'So do you, Cal,' lingering in his wake.

Felicity pulled up outside Luci's the day before Christmas Eve, a bunch of nerves knotting so tight in her stomach she feared it was going to burst open under the tension. Or she was going to throw up.

One or the other.

Callum was leaving tomorrow. In the morning. He'd be back in Sydney by lunchtime.

Out of sight, out of mind, right?

Fourteen hundred kilometres out of sight. Although she doubted even the North Pole would be far enough to keep him out of mind...

She glanced at the lavender growing along Luci's front path. She didn't know why she was here.

No. That was a lie. She knew.

The little farewell party they'd thrown Callum at lunch today just hadn't cut it. Giving him a polite hug goodbye in front of all their colleagues had seemed too impersonal considering what had transpired between them. She wanted to say things to him—personal things. Things she couldn't say in front of everyone at work. But still needed to be said.

Private things.

That she wished him well, that he was going to be all

right. And a brilliant GP. That she was pleased their paths had crossed and there were no hard feelings.

That she'd *never ever* forget their night on the train.

After weeks of keeping every thought and feeling strictly under wraps, she couldn't let him leave without telling him that. She had to *know* he knew.

The last few weeks had been an exercise in self-control and, somehow, she'd managed. *Just*. But with him leaving tomorrow she couldn't deny the strong pull to *see* him one last time.

To just…*look* at him.

So she'd jumped in her car and driven straight here. Hell, she hadn't even bothered getting out of her uniform.

This last time felt ridiculously momentous and Felicity took a deep breath. It caught in the thickening of her throat as her trembling fingers reached for the doorhandle. She fumbled it then stumbled out as if it was her first ever step.

She was hyper-aware of everything around her as her pulse throbbed through her temples. The sun warm on her shoulders, even at almost seven in the evening after a record run of high temperatures and concerns about bush fires. The trill of insects. The laughter of kids somewhere up the street.

The smell of lavender and meat roasting from one of the nearby houses.

'Good evening, Flick.'

Felicity startled at the imperious greeting from behind her, her heart pounding in her chest at being sprung again by Mrs Smith.

Did the woman have some kind of sixth sense? She was only coming to talk, for crying out loud.

'Evening, Mrs Smith,' she said, plastering on a smile as she turned to face the woman who she was quickly coming to think of as her nemesis. Even standing on her footpath in a baggy house dress and hair rollers she somehow still managed to look like the stern teacher who had taught Felicity in grade four.

'You here to see Dr Hollingsworth?'

'Er...' Felicity tried to figure out a response that would cause the least amount of ire from Vickers Hill's self-appointed defender of virtue.

But Mrs Smith didn't wait for any further elaboration. 'He's leaving in the morning.'

'Yes.'

'Back to Sydney.'

'Yes.'

She made a tutting sound. 'You left your run too late, my girl.'

Felicity blinked. 'My...run?'

'He's been here for two months. And you're not getting any younger.'

What the ever-loving hell...? Had Mrs Smith just implied she'd been left on the shelf at the grand age of twenty-eight?

'I'd been married for almost ten years and had three little kiddies by your age. You should be settling down with a nice local boy. What about Ed Dempsey? He's had his eye on you for a while.'

Ed Dempsey? He had his eye on every woman with a pulse. Plus she'd never quite forgiven him for putting a green frog down the back of her shirt when she'd been four.

'There's nothing between Dr Hollingsworth and I.'

'So why are you here on his doorstep at the last minute?' A sudden light dawned over her wrinkly face and Felicity felt nine years old again under her eagle-eyed gaze. 'Ah, I see,' she sniffed. 'You know...' she glanced around her as she made her way towards Felicity '...you can't expect him to buy the cow if he's getting the milk for free.'

Felicity gaped at her old primary school teacher as she contemplated hacking off her ears to unhear what had just been said. *'Mrs Smith.'*

'Oh, you don't think I know what you young people get up to these days?' She stepped off the footpath and Felicity resigned herself to a lecture about the perils of premarital sex from her ex-teacher. 'Why, I...'

She didn't get to finish her sentence and for a brief moment, as Mrs Smith stumbled, relief flowed like coolant through Felicity's system. Unfortunately, she didn't regain her footing and despite Felicity lurching for her as Mrs Smith looked around wild-eyed, desperately trying to grab hold of something, she fell hard on the road on her left side.

She cried out in pain. 'Mrs Smith!' Felicity threw herself down beside her, her annoyance forgotten. 'Are you okay?'

'No,' she managed through clenched teeth, rolling onto her back, groaning in pain as she grabbed her hip. 'I'm not.'

Out of habit, Felicity placed her fingers on the pulse at Mrs Smith's wrist. 'Where are you hurt?'

'It's my damn hip,' she snapped, raising her head as if she'd be able to see a bone sticking out or something before giving up and dropping her head back onto the road on an annoyed hiss.

Felicity was relieved to feel a strong, regular pulse, and slid her hand into Mrs Smith's to give it a squeeze, whether the older woman wanted the comfort or not. She glanced down to find Mrs Smith's left leg was markedly shorter than the right and badly externally rotated. *Damn.* Felicity would bet her life the older woman had sustained a fractured neck of femur.

'Anywhere else?'

'Isn't that enough?' Mrs Smith grouched.

Felicity pressed her lips together to stop herself smiling. 'Okay, hang on a sec.' She pulled her phone out of her back pocket and dialled Callum.

'Felicity?'

She ignored the husky query in his voice. And the tug down deep and low inside her. 'I'm outside. Opposite. At Mrs Smith's. She's had a fall on the road and I'm pretty sure she's fractured her left NOF. Can you give some help, please?'

She could have handled it herself if she'd had to but it made sense to have as much medical support as possible.

'On my way.'

The call was hung up in her ear and she quickly dialled the ambulance station, which, thanks to her home visit schedule, was on speed dial in her contacts. She was ending the call as Callum crossed the road. He was wearing shorts that came to his knees and an ab-hugging T-shirt and was carrying a couple of pillows.

Her heart missed a beat or two.

'You've called an ambulance?' he asked as he knelt on the road, his knees pressing into the bitumen. He didn't look at Felicity as he smiled at the older woman, who was noisily sucking air in and out of her lungs.

'They're ten minutes away.'

He nodded. 'How are you going, Mrs Smith?'

'I've been better,' she said, although the cantankerous edge had obviously been weakened from the pain. 'Think I might have broken my hip.'

'I think you're right,' he murmured, slipping a pillow under her head.

'What's your pain level if one is the mildest and ten is the worst pain you've ever felt?' Felicity asked.

'A hundred,' Mrs Smith panted.

Felicity believed her. Her brow was deeply furrowed and there was a ring of white around her tight mouth. Mrs Smith might be a bit of an old busybody but they bred them tough out here and she was one of the toughest characters in Vickers Hill.

'The ambulance will be here soon,' Callum soothed. 'We'll get you some pain relief and have you on the way to hospital in a jiffy. You think you can hold on for a bit longer?'

'I'll be fine,' she dismissed, her voice gruff, but she squeezed Felicity's hand harder.

Finally he looked at Felicity, their gazes meshing, a question in his eyes she was too afraid to answer.

'We'll support her pelvis in a sling when they get here,' he said, breaking their eye contact. 'I brought out a sheet to fashion one but we'd better wait for the magic green whistle to arrive before we attempt anything.'

'Agreed.' Pain relief was their priority before they attempted any kind of handling. She just wished she could have a magic green whistle for their situation. One that took them back to that night on the train and turned them into two normal people with no baggage and open hearts.

'Did you hit your head, Mrs Smith?' he asked, and Felicity was grateful that Callum's medical training had taken over. Grateful for any distraction from the question she'd seen in his eyes and from the answer she could no longer deny.

Why are you here?
Because I love you.

CHAPTER FOURTEEN

By the time the ambulance had departed it was well and truly dark. Then it was just the two of them standing in the middle of the road bathed in the silent strobing of red and blue lights as they faded down the street. The neighbours who had milled around had since melted away to their homes.

'You want a drink?'

Felicity shook her head. She needed to go now that she knew the answer to the question. She certainly didn't need to drink alcohol around him, lose her inhibitions and blurt it out.

She loved him.

It was insane and the timing sucked. It was too soon and he was leaving—he *had* to leave—but it was there nonetheless. Like a light blinking inside her, sure and steady. She was in deep.

Too deep. Too soon.

And losing him was going to hurt about a thousand times more than losing Ned ever had. No amount of crazy glue was going to put her heart back together after this.

Damn.

'Okay. But I'm assuming there's a reason you came over?'

She nodded. Not that it mattered now. 'No...I just wanted to...say goodbye.'

He shoved his hands on his hips. 'You said goodbye at the party.'

'I know. But...'

'But what?'

Yeah, Flick. But what?

Stupid tears pricked the backs of her eyes and Felicity was grateful for the night. 'I don't know…it felt too public.'

'So come inside.'

She shook her head, standing her ground. 'Here's fine.'

He looked around him pointedly. 'This isn't public? We're in the middle of the street. And…' he smiled suddenly and Felicity's breath hitched '…I'm reasonably certain Mrs Smith has the entire neighbourhood bugged.'

Felicity gave a weak half-smile despite the raging torment kicking up a storm in her gut.

A smile had never hurt so damn much.

She glanced at her car. It was three paces away but her legs were shaking so much it may as well have been on the moon. There just didn't seem to be enough oxygen between them. 'Mrs Smith ruined the mood.'

'She has a habit of doing that.' He regarded her for long moments before holding out his hand. 'Give me your phone.'

She frowned. 'What?'

'You look kind of undecided so let's ask Mike.' He waggled his fingers at her. 'Modern-day coin toss, remember?'

Felicity knew she should just walk away. But he was so damn sexy, smiling down her like that in the dark, being all flirty and charming and reminding her of that night on the train.

Playing dirty, no matter how obvious. And she was weak. No. More than that. Where he was concerned she was *feeble*.

She reached into her back pocket, tapped in her code and handed it over, her fingers trembling almost as much as her legs. He took it, navigating quickly to where he needed to be.

The light from the screen bathed his face in a sexy glow, highlighting his mouth, the dark outline of his whiskers and casting shadows under his chiselled cheekbones.

His gaze met hers as he brought the phone up to his

mouth. 'Mike, should Felicity go to Callum's house for a drink?'

'Are his intentions honourable?'

The stylised British accent seemed loud in the hush that had fallen over the neighbourhood. Felicity's lungs burned as she held her breath and he held her gaze.

'They are, Mike.'

'One drink should be okay.'

He grinned at the quick-fire response as he passed the phone back, his face fading into the night again. 'Mike has spoken.'

Felicity let her breath out in a slow, husky exhalation. 'I think it's time I stopped letting Mike make these kinds of decisions.'

'Oh, I don't know. I think he's been on the money so far.'

Felicity sighed. 'Callum—'

'Oh, come on. Besides, I have a gift for you that I was going to drop off in your mailbox in the morning and now I can give it to you personally.' He put his hand over his heart and added, 'Please...' for good measure.

And not just any old *please*. There was a vibrato to it that floated gossamer fingers around her good sense, wrapping it up in an iron web.

'Okay. Fine. But I'm *not* having a drink. You give me the gift then I'm going.'

He smiled and nodded, clearly pleased with himself. 'Absolutely.'

He led the way up the path lit by subtle solar lamps, the scent of lavender infusing Felicity's senses. It was hard to believe that Luci would be back tomorrow.

God, she had so much to tell her!

Felicity's nerves tangled into a knot as the door clicked shut behind her. 'Come in. Take a seat on the couch. I'll be right back.'

Oh, no. No way was she going to sit on Luci's cosy couch

in her homey living room. She needed to be where she could make a quick escape.

She needed to be *vertical*.

'I'll wait here,' she said, grinding the soles of her sensible work shoes into the parquet floor of the entranceway.

He shrugged. 'Suit yourself.'

Thankfully he was back quickly, placing a package no bigger and sightly bulkier than a business card in the palm of her hand. It was wrapped in pretty flowery tissue paper. 'I couldn't resist it when I saw it in town the other day.' He grinned.

His smile would have been infectious had Felicity not been hyper-aware of the confines of the small alcove in which they stood and the fact the only light in the house was coming from behind them somewhere, which only seemed to enhance his nearness, his broadness, his sexy citrus essence.

She made a concerted effort to concentrate on the wrapping as her fingers fumbled it uselessly. When finally she conquered it she pulled it back to reveal a cheap-looking plastic badge boasting the word *Saint* in tacky diamantés.

'Now it's official,' he teased.

Felicity surprised herself by laughing. She'd been hoping it wasn't something sentimental lest she cry. She needn't have worried. The badge struck just the right note. Light and funny but still sweet and thoughtful.

'You think I should wear it to work?'

'Sure. Here.' He grabbed it from her. 'Let's see if it goes with the uniform.'

'Everything goes with diamantés,' she protested as his plan became clear, but it was too late, he'd stepped right in, opening the back clasp of the badge and fingering the open collar of her polo shirt.

It brought him a hell of a lot closer and she realised she was being hemmed in. The solid door behind her, his solid chest in front of her. Her pulse skipped madly. Goose-bumps swept up and down her neck where his fingers accidentally brushed, rippling out in a hot wave to her breasts, beading her nipples into tight, hard peaks.

'There.' He stepped back but not all the way. He was still closer than he had been.

Closer than was good for her sanity.

'I think it looks perfect.'

Felicity breathed in deep, her oxygen depleted again. 'I doubt Bill would agree.'

'I think Bill would think it was amusing. Angela would think it's hysterical.'

'Yeah.' Knowing both of them, Felicity had to concede the point. 'I guess they would.'

They lapsed into silence, the lightness that had swirled around them moments ago quickly dissipating as awareness of the low light and their closeness set in again.

'So,' he prompted after long moments, 'you came to say goodbye? Before Mrs Smith so inconveniently broke her NOF?'

Felicity fixed her gaze on his shoulder. 'Yes.'

He nodded slowly. 'It's hard to believe it's been two months. It went quickly.'

'Yes.' It had and it hadn't. These last ten minutes, with her chest bursting and her heart breaking and him within touching distance, had felt like an age.

'I guess Meryl was wrong,' he murmured, shoving his hands in his pockets. The action pulled his T-shirt flat against his belly.

Felicity shrugged. Their visit with Meryl seemed a million years ago right now. 'First time for everything.'

More silence. 'I've never really said thank you,' he said, after the silence had stretched about as far as it could without snapping in two. 'The way you took me to task that day. You made me a better doctor.'

Felicity glanced at him, surprised by the statement. But the huskiness in his voice and the earnestness reflected in his gaze showed his sincerity. 'Its fine,' she dismissed. 'You'd been through a lot and you were grieving for your lost career. You'd have figured it out, I'm sure.'

He shook his head. 'No. I don't know that I would have.' He shuffled a little closer, his gaze dropping to her mouth. 'Thank you, Felicity.'

Oh, God. He was going to kiss her. Look away. *Look away.*

He was *thankful* and *grateful*. While she was *in love*. It was all so screwed up.

Look away.

But she couldn't drag her eyes off him. Thankfully, though, she still had some use of her legs and she took a step back. Or tried at least. Her shoulder blades met the door with practically no distance put between them at all.

'I'm going to miss you,' he said, his hand reaching for her, pushing back a chunk of hair that had come loose from her ponytail as they'd treated Mrs Smith, his palm lingering to cup her face. Her eyes fluttered closed. 'Are you going to miss me?'

She was going to miss him with a hunger that would gnaw away at her insides. She just knew it. Breaking up with Ned had been hard—she'd lost a friend as well as a lover. But Callum was an entirely different beast. There'd been no slow build-up to their relationship. No dawning re-alisation. It had been a headlong rush and she'd fallen hard and fast. And that was going to smash through her life like a wrecking ball.

'Yes.'

She didn't trust herself to elaborate as her eyes opened. And then she couldn't, even if she wanted to, because his head was lowering. Slowly. Inexorably.

God…why did she want his lips on hers so *freaking bad*?

'You said your intentions were honourable.'

It was supposed to sound strong, assertive, but came out

all weak and breathy. More a plea than a last-ditch attempt to derail the inevitable.

'They were,' he muttered, his lips almost brushing hers. 'I swear they were.'

And then they were on her and opening over hers, hot and hard and sure, his ragged breath loud in her ears as he demanded entrance to her mouth, his tongue sweeping inside, stroking along hers as his hands went to her waist and his body aligned with hers—hot and hard and sure.

Her pulse hammered and her breath tangled with his as she tried frantically to drag in air. His thigh slid between her legs, pressing in hard, and she moaned as heat flooded her pelvis.

'God...you taste so good,' he murmured against her mouth, and his voice was so deep and dark and needy it filled her head with heat and need and sex. She knew if they didn't stop right now they'd be on the floor in seconds and it wouldn't be sex this time, it would be making *love*, and she couldn't bear for that to be one-sided.

Rallying reserves she hadn't known she had, she tore her mouth from his. 'Callum,' she panted, pushing on his chest, desperate for some distance. 'Stop. Please, stop.'

His mouth was wet and his eyes were a little glazed as he backed up and she breathed more easily. 'Why?' he asked, his hands slipping off her waist, one shoving through his hair.

Because I love you, you idiot. 'Because I can't think, I can't be...rational when you do that. And you're leaving in the morning.'

He gazed at her for long beats before scrubbing a hand over his face. 'Maybe I could stay? I know Meera's back from maternity leave in the New Year but maybe she'd like some more time to be with her baby?'

Felicity blinked. *'What?'* Blind hope surged in her heart even as her head rejected it.

Maybe I could stay?

No. He needed to go. And it was just plain cruel to taunt her with empty possibilities.

He shrugged. 'I like it here. I like working here. I like that *you're* here.'

'No.' She shook her head, hardening her heart, refusing to let herself be carried away by his lust-induced sentiment. 'You can't hide here, Callum. It's bad enough you ran away here.'

He took a step back, clearly surprised by her frankness, although surely he was used to her speaking her mind by now? He shoved a hand on a hip. 'I was after clear air.'

She shrugged. 'You say potato...'

'You ran away too, Felicity, when you came here after Ned.'

'I wasn't running *away*. I was running *to* something.' She shook her head. 'Look...you had this brilliant life and career and you knew what you wanted, then it got blown all to hell. I knew what I wanted too and it also got blown all to hell, but I'm out the other side of it now. You're still in the middle. You said when you first came here that you had something to prove. So go home and prove it,' she said, goading him.

Goading him to leave her.

It hurt, damn it. So *freaking* much.

'Prove that being a GP is what you want.'

'It is what I want,' he snapped.

He turned away from her then, striding into the kitchen behind, placing his fists on the edge of the bench as he reached it. Felicity followed him at a slower pace. His shoulders were hunched, his head hung low between them.

'It's what you want *here*, while you're hiding away in Vickers Hill,' she said, gentler this time, speaking to his back. 'Wanting it *here* is easy. But you have to face the real world, Callum. The people that matter. The only way you're going to know if it's what you *really* want is by going back home. To your *surgeon* parents and your *surgeon* friends and their dinner parties full of shop talk about their latest surgical feats. Because it's only by going back to your old life that you'll know for sure.'

He didn't say anything for a long time. Finally he raised his head and slowly turned to face her. He leaned his butt against the bench and crossed his ankles in a casually deceptive pose but every inch of him was tense. 'Come with me.'

Felicity blinked, her heart beating hard in her chest, as hard as it was bleeding. A part of her wanted to snatch his offer up, throw caution to the wind, just as she'd urged Luci to do.

But this was *love*. And hers was too big to risk on a man still sorting his life out.

She wanted to be with him but she needed to know she wasn't another consolation prize. The consolation woman that came part and parcel with the consolation job.

'No.'

'I like you. I think there's something between us. I think it could be more.'

Felicity sucked in a breath as his rumbled admissions played havoc with her sensibilities. The man obviously knew how to push all her damn buttons. She wondered if he had any idea how much his vague, noncommittal words hurt.

She swallowed. 'No.'

God, how could such a little word be so hard to say?

He cocked an eyebrow. 'You don't want to live in Sydney? I have an apartment on the harbour. And if you're worried about a job—don't be. With your qualifications and experience you could walk into about a dozen jobs straight away.'

'No.' She said it more firmly this time as he didn't seem to be getting the message.

'Why?' he demanded.

'Because you have a lot of things to confront and you don't need me hanging around muddying the waters. You need clear air back in Sydney too. I'm not going to be your distraction. A way for you to avoid facing up to the issues.'

'So you don't think there could be more between us?'

Felicity had told herself she wasn't going to cry when she came here tonight but she was just about at the end of her emotional tether. She wanted nothing more than to take up his offer. If only he knew how much it was killing her to keep denying him.

She cleared her throat of the sudden thickening. 'Of course I do.'

'So come with me,' he repeated. 'Or are you too married to this place to contemplate leaving?'

'No. I don't have a problem with leaving Vickers Hill. I'm just not doing it for someone who's in the middle of figuring out his life.'

'Well, I'm *really* sorry I'm not together enough for you,' he said, sarcasm dripping from every word.

'I don't expect you to be, Callum. I understand you've been through a lot. I'm just saying I'm not getting involved while you're in the middle of it all.'

Felicity rubbed her hands up and down her arms. How could she feel cold when it was still so damn hot?

'There's enough pressure on relationships these days as it is,' she continued, 'and we're not going to survive if somewhere down the track, when you come out the other end of this, you decide that I'm not what you want. That I was just a symptom of your deep unhappiness at the time. One that you're stuck with. I don't want to become collateral damage or be your consolation prize, like becoming a GP was.'

'You would never be that,' he denied quickly, taking a step towards her. *'Never.'*

Felicity took a step back, hardening her heart to the flicker of hurt she saw scurrying across his face. She didn't doubt his sincerity but he still needed time and space, whether he knew it or not.

'Please, just come to Sydney and let's see how things go?'

His words were a cruel blow. *See how things go?* She was in love with him and he wanted to test the waters.

'No.'

'*Damn it*, Felicity. You want to. I can *see* it in your eyes. Why are you being so stubborn?'

Felicity didn't have the emotional energy to go round and round the houses with him. She needed to end it—sever it. Here and now. And she knew just how to do it.

'Because I'm in love with you.' The words came out on a rush of pent-up emotions and clanged into a heap between them. It felt good to get it out even if Callum was staring at her like she'd lost her mind. 'And I want more than "Let's see how things go". You can't give that to me and I'm not settling for less. I'm sure as hell not moving halfway across the country for it.'

He took a step back, looking more and more horrified as his butt met the bench again. 'But…it's only been two months. That's…*crazy*.'

Felicity nodded. 'I know. Trust me, *I know*. But it's there anyway. You want to know something crazier? I think I fell in love with you on the train.'

He took a deep breath and let it escape as he shoved a hand through his hair. 'I…don't know what to say. I really like you, Felicity, I—'

'It's fine,' she interrupted, shaking her head. His horror would be comical if it wasn't currently tearing her heart into tiny little pieces.

She didn't need him trying to stumble through a quantification of how much he *liked* her.

'I know. I understand. Really, I do. But that's why I can't do this. Why I can't move to Sydney with you. And why I'm leaving now.'

He didn't say anything. Just stood there, his face a mix of confusion, shock and disbelief, and all the broken pieces of her heart splintered.

She blinked hard as her emotions threatened to take over.

She needed to get through this without breaking down. 'Thank you for everything,' she said. 'I will *always* remember and cherish our night on the train. And I *will* miss you.' She stopped, cleared the quaver in her voice. 'Have a good life, Callum. Be happy. You deserve it.'

And then, because she really was about to lose it, she turned on her heel and slipped out of the house.

He didn't try and stop her.

CHAPTER FIFTEEN

Two months later...

CALLUM STOOD ON a balcony overlooking Sydney Harbour. Not his. A friend's. Taking a breather from another excruciating dinner party. A murmur of conversation, an occasional laugh and bluesy notes from a top-of-the-range system oozed out into the night air. A light breeze ruffled his hair as the lights on the harbour blurred on the surface of the water courtesy of his compromised night vision.

'Cal?' He turned to find Erica—or maybe it was Angelica?—standing in the doorway, smiling at him. 'Entrées are being served.'

He nodded. 'Okay, thanks. I'll be right in,' he assured, then turned back to the view. He could sense her lingering in the doorway but refused to be hurried. It was rude but he wasn't good company tonight.

He'd told Kim, a thirty-three-year-old mother of four, she had breast cancer today. She'd sat deathly still in the chair as if he'd gutted her while Josh, her husband, had yelled at him then openly wept.

Try as he may, he couldn't get it out of his head. And being here wasn't helping.

Go to dinner parties, Felicity had said. Except tonight he just wanted to be with her. Not at this banal event where everyone was trying to out-surgeon each other. Where they always tried to out-surgeon each other.

It had been hard to start with—reconnecting with the old crowd. And their stories had stirred the old fires, but not like before. He'd spent two years during his GP training burning with envy and resentment that he wasn't in the *club* any more.

And then he'd gone to Vickers Hill…

Why did they keep inviting him back? *Because you keep saying yes, doofus.*

Maybe he needed to say no every now and then. Maybe he needed to start socialising with other GPs. Except not those at his current practice because that wasn't really working out. His billable hours had halved and he'd already had a couple of 'friendly chats' with the head of the practice about picking up the pace.

But how could he have only spent five minutes with Kim and Josh today? Felicity would never have forgiven him.

He'd never have forgiven himself.

God, he missed her. Dreamed about her. Woke up at night aching for her. Had almost called her a dozen times. Had wanted to call her today. To tell her about Kim. To share his utter helplessness and hear the soft note of empathy in her voice.

To hear her say he could do this.

A ferry horn wafted towards him from somewhere on the water and he shook himself out of his funk, throwing back the rest of his whisky and making his way inside.

He took the indicated seat next to another woman whose name he didn't remember. A sumptuous feast was served courtesy of some up-and-coming catering firm in high demand amongst the urban professional set. Absently he wondered what Kim and Josh were eating tonight.

Was it possible to stomach anything after such news?

The talk turned to shop, as it inevitably did, and Callum let it whirl around him. It took a strong stomach to dine with a bunch of surgeons as the nitty-gritty of all kinds of blood, guts and gore was openly discussed.

'What about you, Cal?'

Callum glanced in the direction of the query. It was from

Allan, one of the guys he'd gone to med school with. Allan was a transplant surgeon.

'You save any lives today in the eczema, allergies and asthma trenches?'

There was general laughter. Allan's attitude was typical and one that had dogged and bugged him during his training, but it flowed off him now.

'No. I told a woman she had an aggressive form of breast cancer.'

As a party killer it worked a treat. Callum could almost hear the loud scratching of a needle across a vinyl record as everyone fell silent.

It was bliss for about two point five seconds before Roger, a facio-maxillary surgeon, said, 'You should refer her to Charlie Maddison. He's an excellent breast surgeon.'

'Or Abigail,' Allan added, which garnered a lot of murmured support.

The conversation moved on to breast surgery. No one asked her name, her age or her prognosis. Whether she was married or had kids. Not even the name of the oncologist he'd rung and personally spoken to, arranging for Kim and Josh to go straight there and see her immediately. Nope. They'd moved on to the biggest tumours they'd ever removed.

His phone vibrated in his pocket and he pulled it out, grateful for the interruption, concealing it under the table a little as he glanced at it. He smiled when he saw it was a text from Felicity.

They had been texting back and forth a few times a week for a while now, after some initial radio silence. But with Luci and Seb all loved up and talking wedding bells they'd been included in group texts and it had gone from there.

It wasn't the kind of communication he craved but she seemed to want to keep it light and he was happy for any kind of contact. She usually sent him a picture with Meryl or Alf or any of his other regulars and he'd taken to sending her pictures of the beach and the view from his balcony because a crazy part of him hoped it might just convince her to rock up one day.

Not even her unexpected *I love you* doused that particular fantasy. Not when he missed her so damn much. Okay, it had shocked him at the time but she *had* prewarned him she was that kind of girl.

Callum smiled as he read the text—Mrs Smith says hi— and tapped on the attachment. The image opened up to reveal a selfie of Felicity and Mrs Smith, their faces smooshed together. Felicity was cross-eyed and making a fishy mouth with her lips—so very *Flick*—while the older woman glared suspiciously at the camera.

A niggle took up residence in his chest as he devoured every detail. Felicity had her saint badge on her collar and Mrs Smith was sporting one on her collar too. Her diamantés spelled out *Security*.

He laughed out loud. He couldn't help himself. It was the first time since talking to Kim and Josh he'd been taken out of himself and his lungs suddenly felt too big for his chest.

'You okay, man?' Allan asked.

Callum looked up to find everyone at the table staring at him as if he'd lost his mind.

Maybe he had.

Was he okay? *Hell, no.* If he wasn't very much mistaken, he was heads over heels in love with a chick who'd just sent him a fishy-lipped selfie. The realisation hit him like a tonne of bricks as he glanced at the woman beside him. She was gorgeous and a renal surgeon to boot. But he couldn't imagine her crossing her eyes and scrunching up her face while posing with a cantankerous old woman.

Wow. He was in love with Felicity. He'd been fooling himself that his feelings had been milder, that he'd merely been *missing* her, ignoring the emptiness inside, going through the motions because he'd been determined to prove that he could come back from his injury as if nothing had ever happened.

But it hadn't worked. Because his entire focus was screwed up. Literally and figuratively. He'd been blind to what was important.

Felicity.

The niggle grew to the size of a fist, pushing on his sternum. Who knew love could feel this *bad*? Like a freaking heart attack!

He stood up, pushing his chair back abruptly. What was he doing *here* when she was *there*? Why had he ever left?

Because she'd made him. She'd sent him away. To sort his life out. To work out what he truly wanted.

If you love something, set it free.

Well…mission accomplished. And he didn't want to feel this empty ever again. Felicity filled him up and he didn't want to spend a second longer away from her than he had to.

'Cal? Are you okay?' Allan repeated, his forehead creased.

Callum dumped his napkin on the table. 'I am now, Allan. I'm sorry but I've got to go.'

'Hey, where's the fire?' Erica—Angelica?—joked.

'In Vickers Hill.' He grinned.

Everyone looked a little mystified as he walked away but Callum didn't give a damn as he strode out of the apartment. For the first time in two months—hell, in almost three years—everything felt right.

Felicity had set him free. Because she loved him. Now it was time to go back. Because *he* loved *her*.

It was almost seven when Callum finally caught up with Felicity the next evening. He'd been travelling all day but he felt completely energised. He'd gone straight to her house in his hire car, the speech he'd been rehearsing all day bursting on his tongue, only to be told by a neighbour she was at Luci's, watering the garden.

Callum knew from Seb that Felicity was taking care of Luci's garden while they waited for a buyer in a market that wasn't exactly thriving. Undeterred by the setback, he'd driven straight to Luci's and pulled up outside her house ten minutes later.

He experienced a strange sense of déjà vu as he cut the engine. The street was quiet and the cottage looked as pretty as a picture, the waning sun glowing a lovely honey hue on the brickwork. He half expected Mrs Smith to tap on his window, narrow her eyes at him and call him 'young man.'

He spied Felicity watering the lavender further up the path, her back to him, buds from her phone firmly plugged into her ears. He climbed out of the car and headed towards her, content to stand on the footpath near the front gate and just watch her. Her ponytail swung as she moved her head to whatever beat was being piped into her ears.

A stream of dying sunlight caught the hose spray at the right angle, causing rainbows to dance in the fine mist. She'd told him once that her heart was a pink light glowing inside her and now he knew how she felt as rainbows filled up his chest.

It was a fanciful notion. Utter romantic nonsense. But he didn't care.

She turned then and his breath hitched as she spied him and went very still. 'Callum?'

It wasn't quite the rapturous welcome he'd been dreaming about but it was *Felicity* and he was here with her and that's all that mattered right now. 'Hi.'

She didn't do or say anything for long moments, just stared at him. 'What are you…doing here?'

'I rang Bill last night.'

She eyed him warily as she twisted the nozzle to cut off the spray. 'Why?'

'I asked him for a job.'

'You…did?'

Callum nodded, pleased to hear the first sign of a squeak

in her voice. A good sign, he hoped. 'He offered me his. I'm taking over his share of the practice. He's finally retiring.'

She walked towards him, frowning and nonplussed. 'But…he didn't say anything today.'

'I asked him not to.'

An even bigger frown. 'Why?'

'Because I wanted it to be a surprise.'

She'd reached the gate but kept firmly on her side. 'You did?'

He smiled as her frown lines smoothed out and her tone lightened.

'Yes. I wanted to tell you myself.'

'You did?'

He laughed then. The entire time they'd been acquainted he'd never known her to be monosyllabic. Quite the contrary.

'Yes. Because I love you.' The words came much easier than he'd thought they would. He'd thought saying it for the first time would be terrifying but it was easy.

Things always were when they were right.

'You set me free and you were right to do so. I needed that. I needed to go home to know what I wanted. To be sure. But now I know and I'm back. Because I'm yours. If—' his heart thundered in his chest, suddenly unsure of himself '—you'll have me.'

She stared at him, reaching for the gate and wrapping her fingers around the curved metal. She looked lost for words but the glassiness of her eyes said more than words ever could.

'Felicity?'

'Is it what you want?' she asked, fierce suddenly. *'Really?'*

He nodded. 'It is.' He slid his hand over the top of hers. 'You and me. Here. In Vickers Hill.'

She glanced at their joined hands before returning her gaze to his face. 'What about your job? Your apartment?'

'I resigned today. It wasn't working out there anyway since a bossy nurse taught me patients needed more than five minutes with their doctor. I have to go back for a month and work out my notice but then I'm moving here. And we'll keep my apartment as a holiday home. We can rent it out or leave it empty. I'm sure Seb and Luci wouldn't say no to bunking there while they figure out where they want to be. I know Luci's not keen to have the baby on the boat.'

She smiled then. It was only small but it was progress. 'Seems like you have it all worked out.'

He shook his head. 'No. I don't. Not really. None of it means anything without you and I'm completely terrified now you haven't thrown yourself at me that you've found a six-foot-nine, rugby-playing boyfriend, so can you please just put me out of my misery already?'

Their gazes locked and in that moment he could see love shining in her eyes. Love for him. *Only him.* He hadn't seen anything more beautiful in his life.

She pushed gently on the gate. He stepped back as she stepped through and joined him on the footpath, their bodies almost touching.

'You're the only one for me,' she murmured.

Relief flooded Callum's system. It coursed fast and cool through his chest and flowed hot to his groin. He smiled, slid a hand on her waist, drew her closer, their bodies aligning in perfect synchronicity.

His gaze dropped to her mouth as anticipation tightened his belly.

'Good evening, Dr Hollingsworth,' a familiar authoritative voice said from across the road. 'Flick didn't tell me you were back in town.'

He groaned under his breath and Felicity laughed as he plastered a smile on his face. 'Mrs Smith,' he said. 'I see you've recovered fully.'

'I see you're not back in town for more than five seconds and you're already taking liberties.'

Her disapproving gaze fell to where his body was pressed against Felicity's. *Too damn bad*. There was no way he was stepping away like some guilty schoolboy. Not now he had Felicity exactly where he wanted her.

'Indeed,' he agreed cheerfully. 'And I intend taking liberties as long as Felicity will let me, Mrs Smith, because I love her and she loves me. Consider yourself warned.'

He dipped her then, ignoring both Felicity's surprised squeak and Mrs Smith's scandalised gasp.

'Callum,' Felicity whispered, clutching at his arm while trying not to laugh. 'You're going to give her a heart attack.'

'Lucky for her we know how to do CPR.' He grinned.

Then he kissed her—long and dirty—claiming her mouth with deliberate indecency, giving Mrs Smith something really juicy to gossip about.

Because he didn't care who said what—this was right. This was for ever.

EPILOGUE

One year later...

THEY HELD THE WEDDING in Luci's back garden. Although it wasn't Luci's any more—Callum had bought it the day after he'd dipped Felicity in the street and kissed her, and they'd been happily living in sin together ever since.

Much to Mrs Smith's chagrin.

Seb and Luci and little Eve travelled to Vickers Hill for the wedding. As did Felicity's parents and Bill and Julia, who interrupted their RV trip around Australia.

Felicity wore a pink dress and, thanks to Alf Dunnich, a garland of glorious pink rosebuds in her hair. And, in a few days, they'd be heading to Sydney for two blissful sun-drenched weeks at Callum's apartment where, with any luck, they'd make a honeymoon baby.

The first of many.

Felicity couldn't have been happier as she said, 'I do', and she kissed her new husband in front of all their family and friends.

And somewhere from on high Meryl, who had passed away while Callum had been working out his notice in Sydney, was nodding her head and saying, *I told you so...*

* * * * *

MILLS & BOON®
Hardback – October 2016

ROMANCE

MILLS & BOON®
Large Print – October 2016

ROMANCE

Wallflower, Widow...Wife!	Ann Lethbridge
Bought for the Greek's Revenge	Lynne Graham
An Heir to Make a Marriage	Abby Green
The Greek's Nine-Month Redemption	Maisey Yates
Expecting a Royal Scandal	Caitlin Crews
Return of the Untamed Billionaire	Carol Marinelli
Signed Over to Santino	Maya Blake
Wedded, Bedded, Betrayed	Michelle Smart
The Greek's Nine-Month Surprise	Jennifer Faye
A Baby to Save Their Marriage	Scarlet Wilson
Stranded with Her Rescuer	Nikki Logan
Expecting the Fellani Heir	Lucy Gordon

HISTORICAL

The Many Sins of Cris de Feaux	Louise Allen
Scandal at the Midsummer Ball	Marguerite Kaye & Bronwyn Scott
Marriage Made in Hope	Sophia James
The Highland Laird's Bride	Nicole Locke
An Unsuitable Duchess	Laurie Benson

MEDICAL

Seduced by the Heart Surgeon	Carol Marinelli
Falling for the Single Dad	Emily Forbes
The Fling That Changed Everything	Alison Roberts
A Child to Open Their Hearts	Marion Lennox
The Greek Doctor's Secret Son	Jennifer Taylor
Caught in a Storm of Passion	Lucy Ryder